Sweet Compromises

LOVE HAPPENS • BOOK THREE

SUSAN WARNER

Sweet Compromises

One

Skye O'Malley had been dreading this day. A year ago, her fraternal twin, Stephen, had died in active duty. Today was their twenty-eighth birthday and it was the first she would be spending alone. She was young, single, and she owned her own business, she should have been celebrating. All of her friends had tried to plan something with her today, but Skye had found one excuse after the other to be alone.

She and Stephen had come along late in her parent's life and to have twins was a miracle. They treated them like they were a gift until the day they died. Their parents had passed within hours of each other, after sharing a love that had kept a fifty-year marriage together. She and Stephen had grown up with that example and had vowed never to settle for less. Stephen's nickname for her had been Kitten. He said she was cute but would fight for what she believed in. Skye had said she understood he was doing what he believed in, and that's why she hadn't cried too much when he deployed.

She and Stephen had stayed in their birth home together until Stephen decided to join the Army. Now

Stephen was gone, she was alone in the house she'd grown up in, and for the first time, she was alone on her birthday. She had managed to pull herself out of bed, barely. As she stood in the kitchen looking out the window, she saw someone driving down the lane. Skye put her cup in the sink and prepared to send her well-meaning friend away.

There was a plume of dust being kicked up behind the oncoming vehicle. It wasn't a small car, so that ruled out her best friend, Hannah. It was definitely a truck. She started to pull out the large rollers in her hair and put them in the pockets of her robe. She looked down to make sure her two-piece pink striped pajamas were buttoned up.

As the truck got closer, she saw it wasn't just a truck—it was a monster truck. It looked to be about 150 years old. She didn't have any friends with a truck that big. The gas alone would be ridiculous.

She was at her front door; sure the oncoming person was a salesman of some sort. She held the door open, ready to do battle. When the dark blue truck stopped in front of her house, the windstorm behind it settled down. The door opened and out stepped a man with brown hair that was cut way too short to be stylish. He had a nice build that suggested he either worked out or did manual labor. From looking at his work boots, she assumed the latter. He closed the driver side door and then reached in the backseat, pulling out a duffel bag.

Skye saw him walk towards the door. When he saw her in the doorway, he pulled an envelope from his back pocket. When he was standing in front of her, she recognized him.

"I've seen you in town. In my store," she said.

The man took a deep breath.

"Skye O'Malley, my name is Caleb Matthews, and I have a note to give to you." He dropped the duffel bag and put the note in the other hand while he pulled out his wallet. "But first I wanted to show you that I am who I say I am, and you can hold on to this id if you want." He pulled out a driver's license and his military id card and held it out to her.

Skye looked at the card and shook her head.

"Mr. Matthews, I have to say this is getting weirder and weirder." He didn't seem dangerous, just agitated.

"I have a letter for you."

"So, you said. Can I have it? Who is it from, and why would they send you to personally deliver it?"

He took a deep breath and looked her straight in the eye. "Your brother Stephen."

The words slammed into her as if she had been physically hit. She staggered, and Caleb reached for her.

"Don't you touch me. Who put you up to this? How could you—"

Caleb dropped his duffel. "Listen, I know about Stephen."

Her hurt was replaced by rage. She took a step forward, not caring that Caleb was obviously larger than she was.

"You know about Stephen? How could you know about Stephen? If you knew so much, you'd know—"

"I know he's gone. I was with him when he passed."

Those words took the wind out of her. Her surroundings started to fade, and she had the sensation of falling. Skye waited to feel the hardwood floor come and greet her.

Instead, she heard a man swear and then she was being snatched up.

She heard her front door close and then she felt the couch beneath her.

Slowly opening her eyes, she expected to see Caleb, but she didn't. She could only hear him rattling around in her house. The spigot of water creaked before the water flowed. Moments later he was back with a glass in his hand, sitting her up on the couch so he could give her the water.

"I told him this was going to be a sucky idea, but he wouldn't listen. I told him you'd call the cops and have me arrested for harassment. I tried to convince him this was a really bad idea, but he just kept saying, 'No, I won't leave my Kitten alone on our day.'"

Caleb kept mumbling over how ill-thought out this was, but Skye pushed herself up and looked at Caleb.

"He said what?"

"I told him this was a bad idea."

"Not that part, the part where you said he said something."

Caleb looked confused and then said, "Where he said he wouldn't leave his Kitten alone on our day?"

Skye nodded and then laid down and let the tears flow. "I was his Kitten."

She didn't bawl or cry hysterically. She just let the tears flow down her cheeks.

"I don't know anything else except I'm supposed to deliver this note."

She looked at the note in Caleb's hand and was conflicted. She wanted to see what was in the note, but the memory of Stephen was so close. She warred between needing time to recuperate and needing to know what was in the letter. In the end, it was the need to know that ruled and she took the letter.

She sat up on the couch and held it in her lap.

"Do you want me to leave and come back tomorrow?" Caleb asked.

She looked at him through watery eyes and shook her head no.

"You brought the note, and you didn't need to. I'd appreciate it if you stayed."

With trembling hands, she turned the envelope over and opened it.

Hello Kitten,

Skye's hand went to her mouth, and a moan escaped. She closed her eyes and let the words wash over her and bring back memories. Memories of them playing, picnicking, and camping together. Memories of him alive. With shaky hands, she picked up the letter and read on.

If you're reading this, then I didn't make it. I went to the army to find myself and discover if there was more to life than Sweet Blooms. I discovered that Sweet Blooms wasn't the only thing, but it had what mattered. I've been having a bad feeling I'm going to see mom and dad sooner than I thought. People here are jittery, and jittery people cause accidents.

Anyway, this letter isn't for that. I lived. I loved, and I'm happy with my life. If you have this letter, then let me say Happy Birthday! One of the most amazing people that I've ever met—my best friend, next to you that is—is Caleb Matthews. He's been there for me and helped me through. I know my passing will be hard on you both, and I think the best thing you all can do is celebrate my life so you can both let me go.

You being alone on your birthday isn't the way I want to see you, and I know our parents wouldn't want that either. So, I have one last request to make from you and Caleb. Take the next couple of weeks, share your memories of me, take him to our hidey spots, ask him to sing, and remind each other how much we lived. Then go on with your lives, the both of you. We were twins, but I don't want your body to be walking around and have your spirit with me in the grave.

Tell Caleb and let him stay in my room. He doesn't like people. He doesn't trust easy, and in some ways, he's more fragile than you, Kitten.

I love you, Kitten! We may have been twins, but you were the best of us both. Love hard, so when we meet on the other side, you've got stories to tell me.

Until we meet again,
Stephen "Baby A"

Skye held the letter and let the tears fall. The heat of unshed tears caused her to hiccup. One moment she was reading, and the next tears blinded her. She didn't know when, but she wound up in Caleb's arms as she cried.

Skye couldn't recall how long she had spent crying in his arms, but she knew she had no more tears to give. Pushing away from his chest, she ran her hand through her hair and looked at Caleb. What kind of man was he that he would hold on to a letter for a year, and then deliver it on the right day? Stephen must have meant a lot to him for him to be so dedicated.

That was when Skye made the decision.

She'd follow her twin's last request.

<h1 style="text-align:center">Two</h1>

"I need to walk," Skye announced.

She heard Caleb take a deep sigh before she left the room. She took his sigh as a yes, he would wait for her. Ten minutes later she came back down the steps, fully dressed.

"Ready?" she asked him. Caleb jumped, seeming surprised that he wasn't alone. Skye shook her head and headed out the door.

The morning was almost gone, and the sun was bright and warm. She turned her face up to the sky and let the sunlight refresh her. She tried to think on the bright side. This birthday was definitely going to be memorable, if nothing else. She took stock of what she had. She had the store. She had an amazing best friend, Hannah, and she had a place to live. Obviously, if the note was to be believed, she was also about to gain a roommate.

She started on a path that circled her house, then went through the woods, and came back to her house. She looked at Caleb as he walked beside her. The thing she noticed right away about Caleb Matthews was he didn't make any noise.

"Do you know where you're going or are you just walking around?" he asked as he looked around at their surroundings.

The first response that came to her mind was *Duh! Of course, I know my way around.* There were a lot of choice responses that came to mind, but she couldn't use any of them because, for some reason, her twin had sent this man to her to share memories.

She tried to size him up as they walked. He wore faded jeans and sneakers that had likely seen better days. His shirt was buttoned up to the neck. She remembered the first time she met him at her store, he had a limp. She looked at his leg and then stopped on the path. "Do you want to sit down until I come back?"

He gave her a long look, then tapped his leg and rotated his foot. His dark eyes were unreadable to her, and no expression showed on his face.

"I won't hold you up. We can get started whenever you're ready," he said.

He went to his duffel bag and brought it to the coffee table in front of the couch. He laid out a pocket knife and a small tin case. She needed to think, but maybe this walk would help her to understand what it was Stephen saw that he would send this man to her. She already knew all she needed to know about Stephen.

He stood up and put the knife into a pocket she didn't realize he had on his shirt, and then the tin went into his front shirt pocket. Looking at him only increased her curiosity about the man.

"Despite the weakness you saw earlier in the store, I assure you I won't slow you down on the walk," he said as he waited for her.

"Weakness? I didn't say you had a weakness. I was worried about you."

"You don't need to be."

She didn't know what to say to him after that. She went to the door, and he followed her out. After they had been on the path for a few moments, Skye had to break the silence.

"Do you know what was in the letter?" she asked.

"No."

"You kept it for a year, and you didn't peek at it once?"

"Stephen gave me instructions, and I followed them."

Skye stopped and looked at him, confused. "Was Stephen your boss or some kind of higher rank than you in the army?"

"No, I outranked Stephen."

Skye rolled her eyes. "So are you going to help me at all here?"

"Am I failing to answer your questions?"

"No, you're not. You're just not adding to the conversation."

"There's nothing too relevant to add."

Skye held back an inner groan. How was she supposed to share anything with someone who didn't talk? Ignoring him wasn't an option. Instead, she focused on her surroundings. These were lands where she had grown up. They were filled with trees that didn't look so big anymore, but at one time those trees had served as giants she and Stephen had to slay to save the town. The path she walked on had been a race track on more than one occasion to see who could run the fastest.

Even after Stephen had left, she walked this trail. It brought back memories and made her feel like Stephen wasn't so far away. She closed her eyes and continued her pace. She smiled as the hills and turns of the path guided her. She had forgotten she wasn't alone until she heard Caleb's voice.

"You've been walking this path for a long time."

"It's almost a part of me." She looked at him, and instead of finding him looking at her, his gaze was straight ahead.

"I can tell you watch everything."

"Occupational hazard." He turned to look at her. "I was a sniper in the army. It's hard to complete the mission if you don't know where the target is and how they move."

Skye looked at him and then faced forward. She knew that Stephen worked as a nurse. She couldn't imagine him being friends with someone who didn't value life the same way. She and Stephen cherished life and love. What seemed like a hard request for her to fulfill was becoming an impossible one.

"Did you meet Stephen after the military?"

"No. I met Stephen while I was still active." He glanced at her and cocked his head to the side. "I'm not a member of PETA, and I didn't start out as a pacifist."

She heard the words coming from him but still couldn't really imagine that her Stephen would be friends with someone like Caleb. Confused, she had to ask, "How did you two become friends?"

"I came in one day with a broken arm. I had just finished an assignment but had fallen out of a tree. He was the one they had on staff since the doctor was helping out with others. I was a low priority."

Skye smiled. "There would have been no such thing to Stephen as low priority."

She saw Caleb shrug. "He set my arm and then continued to check up on me. I thought he had been sent by the higher-ups to find out if I was able to keep up. Later on, I realized Stephen wouldn't spy for someone. He would tell me when it was time to go. Eventually, he did."

Skye's grin came back. "He told you it was time to go and get another profession."

Caleb nodded. "He didn't tell me what I did was wrong. He just thought I was losing my edge, and my misses were building up."

Skye shook her head and tried to understand what Caleb was saying. Her brother Stephen had told him to stop because he wasn't good at it anymore?

Caleb continued and interrupted her thoughts. "We'd been talking for a while when he was assigned to the field recruits. The recruits were jittery, and I think we all knew eventually an accident would happen. When it did, I never expected your brother to be the victim. A soldier was running scared, tripped, and his weapon discharged. Your brother was trying to reach him to calm him down, and he was hit."

Skye wrapped her arms around her body and started to walk faster. It was one thing to know Stephen was gone. There were days she still woke up and expected him to be in the kitchen cooking breakfast. She tried to blink away the tears, but no amount of blinking could stop those tears that blurred her vision. An accident. They had given her the official word—in the line of duty. In her head, she had imagined him running out to save someone and getting them to safety and then dying in the effort. But to know he died in an accident. It was wrong. It was unfair. She'd been praying in the day and crying at night. For an accident?

"Why are you here, Caleb? You delivered the news of his death. You gave me the letter. Why are you hanging around?" She knew she would invite him to stay, just to honor her brother's wishes, but Caleb didn't know that. So why was he was still here?

"First off, you don't sound like you should be alone now."

Wiping her tears away with the back of her hand, she stopped and looked at him. "You'll forgive me for saying this, but you don't look like the nurturing type. Knowing your previous line of work, I can't say that gives you a good background on reading someone's emotional state."

Caleb shrugged and nodded his head. "You're probably right, but the second reason I'm hanging around is that Stephen told me to. He said you'd need me. You're right, I don't do emotions. Looking at you crying right now, I'd say your brother knew you pretty well." He kept walking, following the trail and leaving her behind to watch him slowly amble away.

Walking behind him, she had to ask. "What are you going to do for me exactly? Hold my hand when I cry?"

"Nope."

"Make me forget the pain by doing something else?"

"That doesn't sound very healthy, and nope."

She caught up to him and grabbed him by the arm. "What are you going to do then?"

Caleb looked at her and smiled. "Stephen was right. You're pretty persistent." Then he turned and kept walking down the trail.

Skye's mouth was opening and closing like a fish. "What do I say to that, and why won't you answer my question?"

"I was trying to leave before I had to give an answer."

"Do you even have an answer? What are you going to do?"

He walked towards a downed stump and sat down. She stood in front of him before he began.

"I don't like conflict."

"I find that difficult to believe, but what does that have to do with my question?"

He sighed. "I'm going to be here."

She looked at him, speechless. "That's your super-power, your presence?"

"Before you say that has no value, consider the condition I found you in."

"Condition? You came to my house."

Caleb nodded. "I came to your house on your birthday, and what were you doing?"

"Getting coffee?"

"You might have been. What's more important than what you were doing is who you were doing it with."

"I was just waking up!"

"All I know is your brother has been right so far. He said you'd be here alone, and he didn't want that for you."

"I'm alone because I told my friends I needed space!"

"They let you get away with that?"

"Let me—" she said, sputtering. "They didn't let me, I asked for it, and they gave me space. Listen, you might be a great guy, but I don't think I want you here."

Caleb got up and started walking. "If you don't want me here, I get it. I just want you to know I'm not here because Stephen thought you would want me. I'm here because Stephen thought you would need me."

Three

He waited for her on the porch steps. He hadn't waited on the path to find out how she would react to his words. He could only tell her part of the truth anyway. Now he was stretched out trying to relieve the sciatica in his leg. He didn't need to open his eyes to know she was standing near him. He could feel the relief from the sun when her shadow moved over him.

"Did you want to do the job you did?"

He heard the hesitation in her voice, as if mentioning his job was forbidden.

"I wanted to make sure I had a job, and the army found something I was good at."

"Do you have any other skill sets, besides, well, you know, that?"

He opened one eye and looked at her. Hannah had her arms crossed over her chest with her right hand tapping her elbow ever so often.

"The service didn't give me any other skill sets, but I've done other odd jobs before I joined. I'm competent at carpentry, accounting, and I also do some counseling. Stephen convinced me to take some classes in counseling, so I could help others who were displaced. He said if I ever left the military, it would be a good skill. I worked in a cancer rehabilitation center for the last six months, and I did okay. Why?"

She held up her hand. "Let me finish my questions, and then I'll answer yours."

He nodded, but it was just curiosity that had gripped him. He didn't get out of his position and he knew that anyone looking at him would think he was barely listening.

"Did you bring any weapons with you? I'm nervous around guns."

"I have a firearm in my truck, but no, I didn't bring any into your house."

"You're still fit. Do you get the urge to do that anymore?"

Caleb grinned. He couldn't remember the last time someone had said something that would make him break his pose. "Are you asking me if I get the urge to shoot someone? Like a person gets the urge to have a bite of candy?"

"Since you put it like that, yes."

"No, I think I have a better hold on my emotions."

"I'm not sure what you were thinking when you decided to take on this task. I'm thinking you may not fit in while we get this mysterious task done and you make sure my need passes," Skye said, using air quotes when she said the word need. "Everybody knows everybody here, or we know one person who knows that somebody."

"I'm not here for them, and I'm used to not being in the group, so it won't bother me."

She let out a big sigh. "I wanted to talk to you about working at the store with me. It's coming up on the busy time. We're having a festival in about a week, so business picks up at the store. We would be around each other, and you could make sure your conscience is all clear."

He leaned his head on his shoulder and looked at her as she counted off on her fingers all of the reasons why this was a good idea. He wondered what she would say if he told her that when she stood with the sun behind her, the rays framed her face and made her look like an angel. He heard her tapping her foot and was brought back to the question at hand.

"No, thank you," he told her. "Your shop is full of people coming and going."

"I hope so. If not, I wouldn't be making any money."

"I'm saying I don't do well around a lot of people."

He could see the confusion come over her face. "If you don't do well around people, exactly how were you anticipating on helping me remember Stephen? Did you think we'd stay in the house all day long?"

He didn't answer right away. He knew the answer instinctually in his head was wrong, but he couldn't reason out why. So he just blurted out, "Yeah, I did. How long do you need? I thought I'd be here overnight and then you'd be done."

He saw several emotions run across her face—shock, hurt, horror, and then anger. He understood the last one. The other emotions he had no way of addressing. He hoped they'd just pass so he wouldn't have to. When it came to personal relationships he could never apply the rules that he did when he was counseling others. Dealing with his own personal issues could make him forget the basic tenets of counseling.

"If you think I could get over my brother passing in a night, maybe you're not what I need after all."

Skye opened the store from six thirty in the morning until eight at night. She ran the store in shifts with her on the morning shift and her assistant, Cassandra, on the second shift. Like so many, Cassandra Olsen was a woman who had been traveling to find herself, but found herself settling in Sweet Blooms three years ago. Skye knew she was an accountant by trade, but she had settled right in as the store manager.

This morning Skye had opened the store at five in an attempt to avoid Caleb. Before she had left the house she penned a note to leave on the table, telling him thank you for carrying out her brother's wishes, and she wished him the best.

However, when she got down to the kitchen table, a place she was sure he would visit, she saw *he* had already left *her* a note.

Went jogging; will be back in two hours.

She'd grabbed the note and then stamped her feet in frustration. Shaking her head, she'd thrown her note on the table and gone to the store.

By seven thirty, the farmers who had been waiting outside were gone, and tourists and regulars hadn't arrived yet. This was the time she got to straighten the shelves in her general store, do some light maintenance on the shelves. She ran through her mental list, finding calm and centering herself while doing her tasks. Others wouldn't find it exciting stocking daily needs like wire, weed killer, concrete or vitamin supplements for animals but that next to items left in the shop on consignment from local artist helped her to focus.

She was just finishing going through the back rows when she wondered if Caleb had already left. Just then she lifted her head and who should be outside her door but the man in question. Behind him, a small gathering of women and tourists had also stopped. She wondered if he even knew the commotion he was causing. He stood in front of the store window looking in, clearly just coming in from his run. He still had on the sweaty T-shirt that clung to him like a second skin and a pair of grey shorts that showed off muscular legs.

To get her attention, he raised his hand. When his hand went up, so did the side of his T-shirt, giving a glimpse of packed muscles and golden skin. If the shift of women behind him was any indication, the back view of Caleb was just as impressive as the front. He'd been so adamant about not working at the store that she was confused as to why he had come.

She turned away from him and looked at the aisle next to her. She thought for sure he would get the hint and go away. Instead, from the corner of her eye, she could see he had put his hand down but now was waiting outside with his legs shoulder-width apart and his arms crossed behind his back. Again, the crowd was starting to grow behind him. Skye knew she had to do something; otherwise, the women might stampede the store looking at him. She went to the front door and yanked it open.

"Get in." The next second she turned the sign to closed. Then she looked at Caleb and said, "Follow me."

She took him to the back room where they were safe from prying eyes.

"Speak," she said.

"You were right, and I was wrong. You will need more than a day. I want to stay, and I'll work in the store."

She looked into his eyes, waiting to see remorse or guilt, but found nothing.

"I'm glad you realized I was right but—"

"I didn't come to any realizations. I Googled it, and it said there were five stages of grief."

She knew her mouth had fallen open. "Is that your way of saying I was right?"

"I said you were right. I know because I confirmed it."

"You need to work on being wrong, Caleb."

"Actually, I don't think so. It's so rare that I'm wrong that it doesn't seem like it would be worth the effort."

"Are you serious?" she said, then held up her hand to stop his response. "So the store is open; do you want to work here?" she asked quickly before he could say anything else to make her mad. "We start at six-thirty. The pay is minimum wage, but there is commission work on some of the shelves and—"

"I've owned one of these stores before. I know what to do."

"Well, you should've told me I was getting an experienced person. I would have started you earlier."

"Your tone is a little sarcastic. Are you okay?"

"Am I okay?" she said as she choked. "I'm fine. As long as you can get here on time, we'll have no problems."

"Do you think you should start me out on a higher rate?"

"Higher rate? For what?"

The corners of Caleb's mouth went up, transforming his face and making Skye look at him with new awareness. "For being right that you needed me here."

She pushed right past him. "You'll be like every other employee."

"Do you think you'll feel better telling me what to do?"

She grinned and looked at him. "I have to tell you, it does seem appealing." When they both stopped laughing she took a deep breath and gathered her thoughts and courage.

"Listen, I want to thank you for coming out here. I would never have thought you would. The situation we have between us is unique. We'll make the rules up as we go on."

He nodded. "I'll do my best not to be right all the time."

She could feel the steam coming up her neck. This man just had a knack for saying the wrong things.

"Don't stress yourself. You'll start tomorrow."

He gave her a short nod and then headed for the front door and turned. "Stephen said you were a fair person with a good heart. When you realized what the right thing to do was, you'd do it. It might take you a minute to get there because you're stubborn, but you'd do it. I'm glad to see he was right on all fronts."

When the door closed, she fell back against the nearest wall. She saw the wave of people coming toward the door, and groaned just as Cassandra was coming in from the back.

"Skye, are you okay? What happened?"

Skye waved her away. "Can you reopen the store? I just need to collect myself."

To her credit, she didn't question Skye and went to open the doors.

Once Skye was safely alone, she leaned her head against the wall and wrapped her arms around her body. Did she really tell him he could work with her?

They were going to be living together and working together. Last night it seemed so clear. The more time they spent with one another, the quicker he'd be gone. Then she had decided they had said everything they needed to say and she'd send him on his way. Now here she was with a man who got under her skin and made her remember how it was to feel again. She'd taken her feelings shut away for so she wouldn't hurt anymore.

She knew if she stayed in the back much longer, Cassandra would come in. Worse, she might call in their undercover security guard, Peter, to check on her. Cassandra did her best not to mother me and as a result corralled others to help her cause and keep an eye on me. Peter was an older gentleman that everyone knew did security work, even though he was undercover, but he'd been a part of Sweet Blooms as far as she could remember.

He would probably like Caleb, both of them being in the military.

She stood up and pulled herself together. First, she had to be clear. Caleb reminded her of Stephen, that was it. There was no way she felt anything for Mr. I'm Rarely Wrong. She would start planning some things that they could do to fulfill Stephen's request, and Mr. Caleb would soon move along.

Four

Caleb didn't believe in waiting for anything. After seeing Skye this morning and having her confirm he was going to work at the store, he didn't see the sense of waiting until tomorrow. He put on some jeans and a clean short-sleeved denim shirt and went into town.

As he walked up to the store, he could feel the eyes of people staring at him. He knew that in a small town people talked. He also knew that if anyone came into town that not everyone knew, there would be some speculation. On the one hand, he thought it was a great way of defending the town. On the other hand, when he was the cause of the commotion it made him terribly uncomfortable. He tried not to take it personally.

He thought about going back to the house and waiting. In truth, he didn't need this job. Skye hadn't asked, but he didn't need the money. Working as he had for years, he hadn't spent anything and leaving the service on medical, he had all of his benefits. He wasn't a millionaire, but he could live comfortably.

Walking down the block was becoming a circus affair. Caleb was determined not to go back to the house. It felt too much like running. His hand instinctively went to his side, and he had to stop himself from doing a pat down to look for a handy weapon. "Buck up," he muttered to himself.

After watching his steps to make sure he didn't startle anyone, he found himself in front of the store. He could see Skye ringing up some customers. Another woman was working the store, and an older man standing at the door was offering shopping baskets. Caleb took a second look at the way the man moved and could tell he was prior military. As if the man had a second sense, he turned to face Caleb standing on the sidewalk. He looked Caleb over and then nodded to him. Caleb nodded back.

Caleb walked into the store, and a blast of air conditioning hit him. He walked through the aisles watching the customers, and listening. He was listening for her voice. He could hear it through the store. He waited at the end of one aisle, and her laughter floated over the aisles and called him. Her voice washed away the odd feeling he had of others watching him. It calmed him and turned his focus to her.

He stood on the side and watched her take care of the customers. He saw her look to the side and nod at him, then she went back to the register. She talked to each person who came to the register about their purchases, gave them referrals to other stores in town, and then wished them all a good day. Her smile was confident, and she put everyone at ease.

Just as she was finishing up with a customer, the older man from the front waved her over. Caleb followed her. She signaled for another woman to take her place. The older man had a young boy with him who looked nervous. Caleb understood then.

The boy must have been lifting something from the store. It looked like the man had it covered, but Caleb moved near enough to hear and move in case Skye was in trouble.

"What's going on, Robert?" she asked.

"This young man was appropriating some items without paying."

He watched Skye reach out to turn the young man's face to her own. "Billy?"

Robert harumphed. "Aren't you Ms. Waters' son?"

The boy started to squirm. The young man was sixteen and lanky. Before anyone could really start to say anything, he started stuttering. "I-I have money. I was picking up stuff and putting it in my pocket because I didn't want to carry the girly basket."

Robert looked down at the boy. "So when you were going to the door, you just forgot to pay?" he said ominously. Caleb really liked Robert at that moment. The boy squirmed and looked at the door. Caleb looked over his shoulder and saw a bunch of other boys waiting and watching. It became clear that Billy had been sent in to pick up some things from the store as part of a dare. Skye looked over Roberts' shoulders and saw them too.

"Billy, I'm going to let you go." She held up her hand to stop Robert before the first word of protest came from his mouth.

"You are?" the boy asked in disbelief.

"I am. I see your supposed friends are outside. Did they send you in here or was it your idea?" she asked patiently.

"Both," the boy answered sullenly. "I told them I could do it and they gave me a list."

She reached out and tucked his hair behind his ear. "I don't know what it's like to be a sixteen-year-old boy, but I do remember what it was like to be sixteen. I think you need to think about who you hang out with. I'm letting you go, hoping you think about what you're doing. The next person may call your mother or call for the police. You can pay for the items or give them back to Robert. Think on the chance I've given you." With that talk done, she walked away and went back to the register. She didn't call attention to it. She didn't shame the boy or make him feel bad. Caleb thought it was amusing the boy blanched more when Skye had said she'd call his mother.

He watched her return to the register, and her welcoming smile was on her face. The event hadn't changed her disposition. In fact, when a couple of young men came into the shop, she didn't even give them a second look as she helped others in the store.

It was getting close to lunch, and he waited for her to usher the last customers out before closing for lunch. It was just another sign of being in a small town. The stores closed for lunch. After she had smiled, wrapped, and rang up the last customer, she closed the door.

Caleb had been looking at her work the room. How she remembered every person, who came into the store, and for what. He thought about whether he could do that. He'd remember every person who came into the store and what they were wearing. He could probably tell you their height and weight. He didn't know if he could make a difference like she did with her smile and caring attitude. He only thought about getting them to buy.

With the crowd gone, she spotted him and approached. "Cassandra, come over so you can meet a friend of mine."

Cassandra was a cautious woman who came around the counter slowly. "You must be Caleb," she said, holding out her hand. She had a firm grip. Caleb felt like he was being looked over as well as being introduced. "I'm Cassandra, floor help, a part-time accountant, and a stock person," she said with a laugh.

"I'm Caleb, hoping to get a spot here and help you out. If Skye will have me."

Cassandra had dark hair, but he could tell it was color from a bottle. He could tell she was very toned. Caleb knew if he looked a little closer, he'd find a story there.

Giving him a once over, Cassandra said, "If all the gossip is any indication, I'd hire you just for the extra business and lookie-loos you bring to the store. Not that we don't do well, but there was a group of women who bought items just trying to pump me for information about you. If you work here, it'll be like catnip to the masses."

Caleb shrugged. "I want to help out."

He looked towards Skye, and she was looking at Cassandra in shock. "I didn't realize that was the attraction."

He felt Robert before he heard him. "How do you do in tight spaces and lots of people?"

Skye looked at him and shook her head. "You don't have to answer—"

Caleb interrupted her. "I may not like it, but it's a fair question." He turned to face Robert standing by the door. To everyone else, he might have looked like he was relaxed, but Caleb recognized his stance as a preparation to be ready for anything. He didn't like the way this was going, but he was here to complete a task, and he always completed his tasks.

"I won't hurt anyone. I have some points when it gets to be too much, but if that happens here, I know how to go to the back to get away."

"We always have times in the day when we get a rush. I don't want to have to watch the crowd and you."

Caleb nodded. "Understood." Caleb turned towards Skye. "At the end of the day, it's your decision. Let me know." With that, he walked out the front of the store.

Skye stood by the counter, watching Robert. She saw him asking questions, and she was glad. Robert had been in the service and Skye thought he could relate more to Caleb. She could tell Caleb didn't like the questions, but he answered them, and then he left. She thought about how many times people must ask him questions about his time in the service.

Caleb hadn't done anything to make anyone think he was dangerous or had any problems. Skye felt ashamed. She had let her own prejudices run amok. Not every person who joined the military and came out had PTSD or some other kind of problem. She was trying to view Caleb as a different person so she wouldn't have to deal with why he was here. Caleb was here to help her celebrate her brother's last wish.

She needed to give him a chance, and that was why she found herself running out of the store to track him down. He wasn't that hard to find, he stood a head taller than anyone else on the street.

"Caleb? Caleb, wait up," she called out.

He pivoted on one of his heels and turned towards her. "Yes?"

He looked braced for bad information. She smiled and stepped into his personal space, looking up at him. "Let's do lunch."

He looked confused for a moment and then nodded yes. She walked him over to the Banter House, a local eatery where she was working temporarily so she could help out with the upcoming festival. When they arrived, they were led to their seats right away but as she walk across the restaraunt she noticed a gaggle of girls, and thought about leaving.

"Is anything wrong?" Caleb asked.

"No, nothing that wouldn't have to be dealt with either now or later." They sat down in a booth, and she ran her hands through her hair. She didn't know why she did it, Caleb surely wouldn't notice. *When did I even get to the point where I wanted Caleb to notice?*

The hostess, Geeta, came over and took the order quickly. Skye thought she was going to get off scot-free, but it wasn't to be.

Geets repeated the order and then yelled it to the back before settling her gaze back on Skye. "So, Ms. Skye, is this the reason you couldn't come out on your birthday yesterday?"

"No," she answered.

"Yes," Caleb answered.

"Please, you go first," Caleb said to Skye. Skye looked up to a smiling Geeta.

Skye was thrown off by the way he let her speak first but she quickly recovered. "Caleb stopped by my place but we didn't have plans."

"Is that right?"

Caleb agreed. "I can confirm those statements."

Geeta harrumphed. "Well, that was anti-climatic. I was hoping there would be something going on with two fine people like yourselves. Anyway, I can't be right all the time. Have a good lunch."

Skye waited until Geeta was gone. "What kind of response is, 'I can confirm those statements,'" she mocked.

Caleb looked confused. "That was the truth."

"It's a small town, Caleb. I need you to know that if you say you came by, and are now staying at my place, it will look suspicious."

"I am staying in your house, and I'm sleeping under your roof. If that looks suspicious, we'd better get ahead of the game and tell them we are staying at your house."

Just when Skye was going to explain, Geeta showed up again. She held out her hand to Caleb. "I'm Geeta. I'm everyone's mother in town. Since you're staying in Sweet Blooms, I have to know… Are you here to bother my sweet Skye?"

Caleb gave a long look to Geeta. "I'm not here to bother her. I'm here to heal her."

Geeta was Sweet Blooms woman on the hill. She had wisdom beyond measure and she was old enough to not have to worry about how she said things. Geeta gave him a returning long look. "Yes, I believe you are, but I can also tell that might not be the only thing you heal."

If it were possible, Skye would have fallen through the floor into the basement. Trying to pull the awkwardness away from the moment, Skye interrupted. "Caleb is going to work at the store with me so I thought we would celebrate with some ice cream. Two scoops of french vanilla and chocolate chip cookie dough with whipped cream and cherries on them."

Geeta didn't scribble the order; instead, she yelled it over her shoulder. Then she reached out to Caleb and patted him on the hand. "I hope you find the dream you're looking for, boy."

"Sorry, I forgot how Geeta is everyone's mom. Everyone thinks she's like that because she's had a lot of miscarriages and, as a result, takes care of everyone else."

Caleb leaned back in the booth. "I like her. I like Robert too."

"You weren't insulted by Robert's questions?"

"No, I was grateful that you had someone around who could ask those questions and look out for your safety."

"Caleb, I won't ever get you." Before she could clear up her confusion, the ice cream came.

The young waitress set the ice cream in front of them and Skye watched Caleb as he sized up the dessert and looked skeptically at the cherry on top.

"You have eaten ice cream before, yes?" she teased.

He turned the small bowl around. "I have eaten ice cream before, but not with whipped cream and a cherry on it. Do you want it?" he offered.

Skye smiled. "This is how Stephen and I celebrated a new job or good news. Ice cream is a little decadent, and the whipped cream is homemade here. The cherry is mine, though. Thank you for recognizing that," she said as she plucked the cherry off the top.

He still looked confused.

"Go ahead, Caleb, taste the whipped cream."

He looked at her skeptically. "It doesn't look like it has any nutritional value."

Skye laughed. "I can pretty much guarantee it has no nutritional value at all but it tastes amazing."

Caleb kept sizing it up. "I'd probably have to run an extra thirty minutes to—"

Skye reached over, scooped some whipped cream, and held it in front of his mouth. "Come on, Caleb, try it. Trust me and try it just once?"

His eyes locked with hers, and what started out as a fun moment had become more personal. He held her gaze as he took a taste from her spoon. When he had taken the sample from her spoon, he closed his eyes and swallowed. Skye looked at him, watching all of his emotions run across his face. When he opened his eyes, his smile was broad.

"You were right, it's good, and it might even be worth the extra thirty minutes of running."

Skye sat back, feeling as though she had just crossed a mountain and made it to the top. She shifted in her seat. The silence as Caleb demolished the ice cream was more personal than feeding him. What had she been thinking to feed him in public? Okay, what had she been thinking about feeding him at all?

"If you want to be around people, you have to be open to trying new things," she said. "If you just stand around and be all broody and silent, then people will assume whatever it is they think must be correct. It's odd how people are comfortable when they put you in a box. Then you have to work twice as hard to get out of it."

Skye knew everyone thought she came from a happy home with a wonderful twin and that she was happy all the time. When she wasn't happy, it was almost always a problem. No one could wrap their heads around the idea that she could not have a perfect life.

Caleb sat back in the booth and gave her a long look. "You're right."

She smiled at him. "What? Are you saying someone besides you could be right?"

"Yes, other people are right as well. That has no bearing on my high percentage of being right most of the time. Thank you."

"For?"

"For taking the time to say something. I know this whole thing hasn't been easy for you. I know I'm not the easiest person to be around, but you've been adapting well."

She looked at his smile, and it crossed her mind that when Caleb smiled, he was attractive and sexy in an awesome kind of way. It made her feel that tingle in her stomach that was more than just butterflies.

She pulled her ice cream bowl closer and began to clear out the little bowl. She looked up and found Caleb staring at her.

"What? Is there whipped cream on my cheek?"

"No, I just keep thinking about the way Stephen talked about you. He was right about so many things, and it amazes me."

Skye let out a deep breath. "We haven't really talked about Stephen and what we're going to do, and I think we should."

"I have. I think it's your turn, Skye. What you see is what you get with me. I'm not sure what kind of memories you have with Stephen."

"Do you have any siblings?" She blurted out the question before she could stop herself.

"I don't have any siblings I know about."

"Well, that's an odd statement. Could you be any more mysterious?"

"I spent a lot of time in foster care. My mother had some mental issues that made it difficult for her to take care of me. I was the first born, but I heard she had tried to get better and got married again."

"You didn't go back and see her?"

"By the time I found out, I was already signed up for the service. There had been so much time between us. I didn't go looking for her, and she didn't come looking for me."

"I can't imagine not having a family."

"I can't imagine having one that stays around."

Skye gave a sad smile. "Well, we're going to make an odd pair in this celebration."

Geeta brought the bill. Caleb grabbed it before Skye could even reach across the table.

"I'm paying," he said.

"I'm liking a man who pays, shows up on a woman's birthday, and looks fit in a pair of sweats," Geeta said.

Caleb smiled. "Thank you."

Geeta smiled and patted him on the shoulder. "You're good stock. Skye needs a knight."

When she left the table, Caleb looked at Skye. "Do you need a knight?"

Skye heard the question and tried to think of something witty and worldly to say. Instead, what came out of her mouth was too close to the truth. "I thought I did, and if you're it, your armor isn't as shiny as I thought it would be."

"The rich knights had armor. I'm afraid I've just got a hard head. Thanks for bringing me here," he said.

Skye looked at the table and saw he had thrown

down some extra bills as a tip. "If you keep leaving tips like that, no one will believe you're from the poor side of knights."

"I believe in rewarding for good service."

Skye rolled her eyes. "I should have known it would come back to service with you."

They both stood up, and after she had pulled her sweater around her, he picked up her hand. He looked intently at her hand for a moment and then slowly placed a kiss upon it.

"I'm not a knight with anything to offer but my thanks," he murmured. She was shell shocked and followed him as he placed his hand on the small of her back and guided her out of the restaurant. On the sidewalk, he said he was going home to work off the ice cream. Skye remembered nodding and waving him off and then just standing there.

Her hand was still warm from the feel of his lips pressed against her skin. Caleb was not like the men her mother told her about in stories. She knew the signs because she'd been waiting for them all along. The tingles in her stomach, the giddiness when he came near. The urge to simultaneously play with and discover new things with a person. Her mother had told her it happened fast and just felt right with no reason or explanation. She hadn't told her the person who would make her feel like this could be from a place that was so emotionally void compared to her own background. She hadn't explained that her knight on a white horse might be a beat soldier who never stood in the light.

How could she be attracted to an attractive man who was her emotional polar opposite?

After the store closed, Hannah Jenkins—her best friend who was recently engaged to Adam Cade, a Sweet Blooms guy who did well in the city and returned home—called her to have dinner. She called Caleb to let him know she would be out late. He told her no problem, they'd meet up in the morning when he started work. It was odd when she finished the call how natural it was. When she made it to Banter House, she saw Hannah sitting in a booth, glowing.

"Well, I don't have to ask how are things between you and Adam," Skye said.

"You know Adam is going all out trying to get his house built and then the woodworking shop. I think he may be having some issues with the shop and Pierce, but we'll have to wait and see." Hannah waved her finger at Skye. "Don't try and change the focus of this meeting. I want you to know I'm hurt and offended."

Skye watched Hannah put her hand to her chest in mock distress.

"Okay, Hannah, please tell me what I have done to bring this on."

"You can't know how left out I felt when I found out my friend was involved with a very hot man named Caleb. I've met Caleb, and if I weren't totally gone with Adam, he'd be a good catch. How could it be that my best friend couldn't tell me that she wasn't coming out on her birthday because she was spending it with a mysterious buff man? And then to have to hear it from Nathan, my son! Billy told him because he had a run-in at the store that he was very vague about, but he said besides scary Roberts at the door, there was another giant of a man who was protecting my friend."

Skye heard all Hannah said and then had to cover her mouth to stop the loud laugh that threatened to escape.

"First of all, you make it sound like I've been hiding Caleb. I haven't. He came to me on my birthday."

"Skye, he came with Henry. I've seen him in town. I thought you two had already met before."

Skye shook her head. "No, I hadn't met him. He drove up to the house on my birthday and said he had a note from Stephen."

Hannah reached out and touched her hand. "Oh, no."

Skye gripped Hannah's hand. "He wasn't crazy. He did have a letter from Stephen. I have to tell you, at first I felt like the world was caving in on me. I thought for sure he was crazy. He's military, so that gave him some credibility, but he was a sniper or something. I'm thinking, why would Stephen be with friends him? It's against everything we believe in. He was a nurse, for goodness' sake."

"And now?"

"Now I'm confused. Stephen sent him on my birthday to see if I had moved on. Stephen was right; I hadn't. He thought me and Caleb having a last hoorah of memories would help me heal."

"It's only day two, but how's it going?"

Skye pulled her hands back and leaned into the booth.

"Caleb is a different animal. He's a different kind of man than I'm used to. I feel like the things we would have to say about Stephen say so much about ourselves. I know we are supposed to be letting go of Stephen, but this feels like so much more."

"More like white horse and carriage, or more like run away to Vegas and what happens in Vegas stays in Vegas?"

Skye laughed. "Definitely not a Vegas situation. Caleb, for all of his experience and the places he's been and his worldliness, doesn't know any of the things I take for granted about people and kindness and the simple pleasures of life."

"I'm looking at you, Skye. I see stars in your eyes for a man you've just met. Are you sure you're falling for him or are you just trying to hold on to someone who knew Stephen? It's no secret you two were twins, and you were close. It was hard on you when he left to go to the military, and it was even harder when they told you he had died in the line of duty. Are you sure you're holding on to the living or the dead?"

Skye looked her best friend in the eye. "I'm scared, Hannah. I'm scared that I'm holding on to the living and he's not what I expected at all. Like he says, he's no knight in shining armor."

"Well, as long as we know it's Caleb, let me give you some advice. Throw away the knight in shining armor dream. I found a lot of knights who had shiny armor, and they were aluminum. They didn't know how to stick around, and they didn't fight for anything. If it's true, then hold on, and you and Caleb will work it out."

"If it's not?"

"I'll be here no matter what. We'll look at this months later and say he was the one, or we'll be here a month later and say candy looks good but it's bad for the teeth."

Skye laughed. "Where do you get these expressions?"

"It's Delilah, Adam Cade's grandmother and all knowing matriarch with the sweetest heart. She knows tons of them, and she visits us more often now. Since Adam is funding a large part of the festival this year, she's taking a bigger part of the planning committee."

Skye shook her head and looked around the restaurant. "Let's get food. I'm famished. Besides, I have all day to work with Caleb tomorrow."

"All day?"

"That's right. I didn't tell you. I had a moment of craziness and gave him a job at the store, thinking the more time we had, the sooner he'd be gone."

Hannah laughed. "Okay, this story I've got to hear, but food first."

Five

"So much for the bags of feed lined up on a makeshift dock," Caleb said, looking at the rear entrance of the store.

"I know we're a small town, but we do know what the internet is. The suppliers will deliver directly to the homes that are on the outer roads, so we don't have to worry about it." Skye opened up the back door, and they walked into the storage area. "I'm glad we don't store feed. Can you imagine the mice—or even worse, rats— that would attract?"

"What's a little pestilence, to keep to the old ways and tradition?"

"Huh, do you not recall the black plague or do you think we're exempt from it?"

"Isn't this the part when I say, it's when women were women and men were men. Signalling I have no clue about what's going on in the world or how to answer the question."

Skye looked over her shoulder and grinned.

"Well, in this age of emancipated women, we still don't do pestilence." She turned on the lights, and the room was large with the walls filled with supplies.

In the middle of the room was a work table that was set up like an island, and on it were some supplies that needed to be put up.

This morning they had both left in her car. Skye wanted to get to the shop early to show him how it was set up and where everything was. He'd already been in the front of the shop and the back just had two rooms. The room he was in now had a set of stairs that went to the basement. She kept bottles and nonperishables down there.

She pointed towards the staircase. "The basement. I keep long term supplies like glass, display cases, shelves, and other furniture that isn't wood. Also, in the basement are temporary sleeping digs. It doesn't happen often, but if there's a storm, I'll sleep here. If someone comes and they make it to the store, I'll be able to give them supplies they may need. We haven't really had anything like that, but it serves as a bunker if we get tornados or hurricanes as well."

"You know it's not too late. You can go back to the house, and I'll meet you later, and we can make up a schedule then if you're still not feeling very comfortable," she said.

"No, you were right at lunch yesterday. I do need to meet people more and get out. I want to try some new things. Maybe they'll all be as good as whipped cream on ice cream." He knew this would be the best way to share with Skye. Ever since he had tasted the ice cream, he wanted to know what else Skye could show him. Stephen had warned him as well that he needed to be open to new things.

She smiled at him and walked out to the front of the store. "I wouldn't have thought you could before, but I the ice cream did give me hope. Robert is a lot like you. If he can do it, so can you."

"Thanks, I think?"

She tapped her chin thoughtfully, an action that him thinking the word *adorable*—a word he was certain he had never used before in his life. "I think we should have a signal between us if either of us thinks there's a problem."

"Do you have it with anyone else?" he asked.

"No, but I think for the first couple of days if you feel like you have a new situation that's not going well, or I feel that way, we can signal each other without making a big deal."

Caleb gave her a second look and then agreed. He was touched—another word he'd never used—by the thoughtfulness of the idea. "Okay, what's the signal?"

Skye nibbled on her lip as she thought about it. He tried not to watch the action too intently.

"How about you lift your hand? You're tall enough that if you do, I'll definitely see it from anywhere in the store."

Caleb looked around the store. "I don't know, Skye, maybe a whistle will do better?"

Skye laughed. "Don't joke! Let's do the raised hand thing. If you see my hand raised you'll know I need you. If I see your hand raised I'll know you need me to come to you."

Skye looked at the front door and noticed there was a line of people already starting to form. She peered back at him as she moved to the door.

"Here's your last chance to run away," she teased.

He stood with his arms crossed over his chest. "Open the door. I didn't run from enemy forces, and I won't run from a bunch of older ladies or tourists."

Laughing, her brown eyes dancing, Skye turned the closed sign to open. "They all start strong. Just you wait and see."

"Open up the doors. Let me show you how it's done." There it was. Him joking with another person, much less a woman. She had a gift when it came to coaxing the emotion from him. It wasn't a duty. He didn't feel obligated. He just wanted to be with her. When she turned away, he kept the smile plastered on his face.

A better woman you'll never meet. He remembered when Stephen had said that. Caleb had thought he was blinded by having a twin. Now he knew different. Skye made him notice the sun again. She made him want to participate in life again. She made him want to try to be that knight he knew she deserved.

He let the people swarm in and then started taking note of where each one was and where Skye was. He had told her the truth. He had been in foreign countries and in unnamed lands. Looking back on all of the missions he had ever been on, he could say with clear conviction that this assignment was the most dangerous. If he stayed too long, Skye would find her way into his heart.

"Thanks for taking lunch with me," Robert said as he took a seat on the curb in the back of the general store. "It's not fancy digs, but I didn't think you'd mind."

Caleb nodded. "I didn't think this was about the food."

"You thought right." Robert paused and gave Caleb a hard stare. "What are you doing here?"

"Fulfilling a last request."

"I heard that part of the story. You don't need to work here to do that. In fact, if you kept to the letter of the request, you should have been gone."

Caleb flexed his shoulders and let the tension run out of them. "No disrespect intended, but am I the one you should be talking to? I know Skye is more than old enough, and her parents are deceased. Everything that I've done so far has been with her consent and even encouragement."

Robert gave him a smile that had no warmth. "Skye has been living here in Sweet Blooms all her life. You could get her to agree to anything and make her think it was her idea. She's not built like we are. She's better, and she deserves better than you."

Caleb nodded. "You're right; she deserves better."

Skye poked her head out the back door.

"Gentlemen, I'm going to make a run to Lucy's place. She needs some things, and she's a little short-handed today, so I'm going to drop them off. I'll be back before lunch ends."

Both of the men looked at her, and neither got a chance to get a word in. One minute she was there and the next minute she was gone.

"That's Skye. She'd do whatever a person asked her. I've watched her grow up here, and I'm concerned when she hangs around a person like you."

Caleb thought about what Robert was saying. He didn't take it personally because it was the truth. He could think of no other situation, save for the one they were in now, where he and Skye would ever come into contact. He supposed if he were looking at it from Robert's side, it would seem like he was bad news for Skye.

Caleb had settled himself with the idea that he was going to be alone. He thought no one would be able to put up with him. It wouldn't be fair because he would never change. Stephen had started to sell him on the idea of family, and then he died. Caleb thought it must have happened during one of the many conversations with Stephen that his mind was at least open to the possibility of being with someone.

The stories that Stephen had told about Skye seemed so exaggerated that Caleb had allowed himself the indulgence of thinking that if such a woman existed he would give it a try. She would be a woman who was worth trying for. When he had first arrived in Sweet Blooms, he saw the drama and problems that Henry had with his son. No, he hadn't changed his mind about children as of yet.

When he finally met Skye, he could say the idea of a partner didn't seem so far-fetched. It was all still a dream until he started to talk to her and work with her.

Earlier that day, or maybe it was the ice cream at Banter House, he'd made a decision. He was always honest with himself, and the truth was that he wasn't here just for Stephen—he was here for himself as well.

"I'm going to give it a try. I've got challenges. I need to know if she wants to try to work on my broken parts," he said. He didn't believe in miracles, but when a perfect shot came by, he believed in taking it. Skye O'Malley was that perfect shot.

"I can't say I agree because I think she's too good for you. I know her parents are gone, but I've set myself to look after the women in this shop. I wanted to make sure I knew what to do with you."

"What to do with me?" Caleb grinned.

"Yeah, I figured if you went missing, no one would be the wiser."

"Are you thinking you can take me, Robert?" Caleb asked.

"See, boy, that's where I got you. If you're going to be with Skye, you better get used to the way things happen here in Sweet Blooms. It's not the frontal attacks that get you. It's those side swipes that just catch you totally unaware."

Caleb looked at Robert, who seemed to be looking far away.

"You talking from experience?"

Robert nodded. "I don't know what it is, but you'll find that love can side-swipe you in an instant here in Sweet Blooms. Are you going to go after her?"

Robert sighed. "There's history in my story, but to answer your question, yes, I'm going to go after her. The question is, will she have me?"

Caleb had been all through Skye's house. He'd done it the first night so he would understand how many ways there were to get in and out of the building. However he hadn't really spent any time on the porch. It was an odd porch because it was on the back of the house instead of the front.

Skye had asked him to meet her here before she left the store. He didn't know what it was about, but he wasn't very optimistic after the meeting with Robert. Still, after the conversation with Robert, it was probably a good time to talk to her. To get an idea if she was even open to the idea of trying with someone like him.

He was sitting on the swing thinking maybe he had messed up the message or somehow had misinterpreted what she had to say. He stood up, about to go in the house, when Skye popped out with a smile on her face.

"Great! You're already here. Take a seat."

Her voice sounded high and nervous. He stood, waiting for her to sit.

"Please sit." She gestured toward the swing. Her speech was fast, and again he wondered if this conversation was going to be more of the *pack your things, I don't need you in my life to remember my brother* sort of thing. Those words coming from her would have some kick, but he'd move on.

"Are you okay?" he asked.

"Great! I'm just a little scatterbrained right now, but I'm sure it'll get better." When she seemed to notice he had taken a seat, she sat down.

He was on the other side of the swing, and it began to sway with a gentle rhythm. He could see she was wringing her hands and licking her lips. He didn't know what it was, but he figured the best thing he could do for her right now was to give her some time and space.

"Why don't we talk later?" he said as he stood.

"No, please stay," she said, reaching out to grab his arm. She looked down and seemed to realize she was touching him and she retracted her hand.

"What I want to say is that I would like to have a conversation with you. If you're not up to it, I understand."

"Skye, are you in trouble? Do we need to leave?"

She looked at him, and her normally clear brown eyes were filled with worry and doubt.

"Hey, Skye, tell me. Is there something you need?"

She gave a short laugh. "It's funny you say that

because, as it turns out, there is something I need. I-I mean, I'm not going to die or anything. And when I say I need it, I really mean that it's been something I have been looking for all my life, so I guess I need it if you think about it like that."

Caleb reached out and touched her knee and smiled. "Ask me, and it's yours."

"Really? Is it really that simple?"

"Yes," Caleb replied. He couldn't stand seeing her like this. At least he knew whatever it was, it was something he could potentially give her. It took his stress level down a notch or two. Seeing her so nervous, he started thinking about how much cash he could get and how soon he could get them out of the country. Then he paused and remembered he was with Skye, and this was Sweet Blooms.

"I want to ask you something and explain something, and I don't know where to start," Skye said as she twisted her hands.

"Okay, I usually find the easiest way to deal with things is to deal with the goal first."

Skye nodded her head with him. "Goal first," she parroted. He caught her gaze and reached out to hold her hand.

"I've got you, Skye. Let's do goal first."

"Goal first. Well, goal first, you say."

"Yes, what do you want?"

Skye scrunched up her nose as if she were smelling something distasteful. "Who does things backward like this? It seems like I should work up to it."

Caleb had to take a breath. In a matter of minutes, she went from extremely nervous to dissecting perfectly good instructions on how to address the situation.

"If you do the build-up first, it will seem bigger than it is," he counseled with all the calm and patience he could find.

"Well, it is big, otherwise, I wouldn't have an issue."

"Skye?"

"Goal first. That has got to be the silliest thing I've ever heard."

"Skye?" he said, prolonging the last syllable of her name.

"Big things deserve their place and—"

"Skye, tell me already!"

"I'm trying to figure out if I should have a relationship with you. There, that's the goal first." After the words had left her mouth, her hands went over her mouth. "You ruined it!"

She got ready to stand up, and he reached out and held both of her hands. "Please, Skye."

The words didn't take the heat from her face, but it got her to sit back down on the swing.

"Now that you've ruined it, I can tell you the rest," she said with a long, drawn-out sigh. Caleb wasn't sure he could hear the rest. Here he was preparing to walk away from perfection on her say so, and she was here to give him a chance.

"I know we have to carry out Stephen's wishes. I need to make sure I like you, and that I'm not holding on to my twin. I'm pretty sure which one it is, but it never hurts to test these things."

Caleb nodded. She didn't know she could have said anything, and he would have agreed. He was trying to understand that she wanted to see if she could be with him.

"I need to be around people, Caleb," she said firmly.

"So this thing you have about not being around people is something we have to work on."

"I can do that."

"You barely made it in the store today. How can you say you can do that?"

"Because I think the goal is worth it," he said quietly. Skye stopped and looked at him. He could see her blinking back tears.

"I have to tell you about the dream first and then let's see if you're still on board?"

"Go ahead, but I can tell you now there is nothing you can say that will make me change my mind. If you hadn't said anything today, I would have said something."

Her eyes were so wide they turned into saucers. He would have thought it was funny if this moment wasn't so important in his life.

"Well…that's good to know," she said with a smile that took away some of her worry lines and tension in her body. "Why?"

"Why what?"

"Why were you going to have this talk with me?" She asked in a soft voice, leaning a little closer to him.

"It seems as though if I didn't, Robert might attempt to follow throught with a barely veiled threat to beat me to save you, and that wouldn't go well for anyone."

"What?" Skye snatched her hands back and sprang up from the swing. "You see, it's things like this that make me think this is a big mistake!"

Caleb was confused. "What's wrong?"

She looked at him and then plopped down on the swing. She looked so defeated, and Caleb felt powerless.

"Skye, if you tell me the problem, I'll try to fix it, but I can't do anything if you won't tell me."

He could see she looked miserable, and he wasn't sure how but he knew he was the cause.

"The problem is my parents had a perfect marriage. They met each other in high school and got married right after and lived in Sweet Blooms. Both of them decided to open the store, and they loved it. The only other thing they ever wanted was kids. In a first and last attempt—they tried when the doctors claimed my mom would have been too old—they were blessed with twins.

My brother and I grew up around the most stable, loving people in the world. They were patient, and every day they told us how we were their miracle. We grew up thinking we'd meet someone just like our parents did. We'd find true love and live happily ever after in Sweet Blooms."

Caleb sat back in the swing and listened. When she was done, the enormity of their problem hit him like a ton of bricks.

"Skye, I wish I had the nice story you had. I wish I could tell you my parents were thrilled when I came. The truth of it is, my mother was always mentally ill. I'm not sure I could name my father, and I grew up on the street and in foster homes.

"I never really believed in marriage or forever. I knew too many guys who had a woman in every port. I knew too many women who were looking to trap men who had on a uniform."

Skye looked towards him. "I'm looking for a white knight who wants to stay here in Sweet Blooms. I wanted to see if you were that one."

Caleb cleared his throat, and he stood up and looked at Skye. She wasn't smiling, and she looked kind of depressed, but she still looked amazing to him.

"I can't tell you that I'm a white knight or prince charming for anyone, much less someone as decent as you," he said as he walked away. Then he stopped at the door to the house and looked back at her. "What I will say is, I'll give it a shot for a chance to be with you, if you're up for it?"

He saw her turn around in the swing and face him.

"Really? Do you think we have a chance?"

"I don't know. What I do know is I've never thought about being with anyone long term until you, and if that's what it feels like to be in a relationship, I'll give it a chance."

Skye smiled. "So you're up for becoming a white knight?"

Caleb smiled. "I can already slay dragons. But I think you need to work on acknowledging that I'm right. Just like I told you when I first met you."

Skye shook her head. "You've been hit upside the head too many times."

Both of them laughed. Caleb tipped his head to her. "Until the morning, damsel in distress."

Skye rolled her eyes. "I can see you're going to make me pay for telling you about the knight. Whatever, go clean your armor. I'll see you bright and early at the store."

Caleb left and went upstairs. He counted the steps so he wouldn't run. She was going to give him a chance. That's all he needed. Stephen was right when he said Skye would make him believe in people again.

Six

Caleb was used to working out. He was used to running for miles with packs on his back. He could deadlift his bodyweight or the weight of the heaviest team member before he went on assignment. So he knew he was fit. He ate healthy—in fact most people would call his a bland diet. He was used to sleeping in three to four-hour increments.

The store was a whole new experience. This didn't require brute strength or patience. The store required endurance. Caleb was surprised to find that today was Skye's day off, but he took it in stride. Cassandra could compete with any drill sergeant he had ever had. She had eyes in the back of her head, and nothing got past her.

It was seven thirty and the morning crowd had already come in. The store opened at six thirty to locals who knew better. The store stocked everything from grocery goods that local shops bought in the event of shortages, as well as physical building equipment. He was restocking shelves almost as quickly as they were being emptied. Just when he thought it was almost done, Cassandra came out with what she called the consignment shipment.

He had to sort, tag, and display the new shipment. She had just given him a quick tutorial on display formats when the bell rang, and the race was on again as people came in. At one point he had put the box down because a customer needed help. When he was done, he couldn't recall where he had put the box. Robert gave him a grin and pointed him toward the corner. Caleb nodded to him and went to retrieve the box.

By the time lunchtime came, Caleb was ready to get a bit of fresh air. Unfortunately, air was not on the schedule for drill sergeant Cassandra. There was a convention of knitters and crocheters coming into the town, and she wanted to put up a welcome sign and rearrange the store so they could have a corner and buy some items that had been ordered for them. By the time they had finished creating her "vision" and giving it the right "feel," it was time to open, and lunch was over.

It was still a bit of a surprise that both Skye and Stephen grew up in this atmosphere. Stephen had described them as the darlings of the town. The miracle children born to the perfect pair. He was glad there was so much work to be done. With so much work, he didn't have time to overthink why Skye hadn't told him today was her day off.

He liked being around Skye, and he had gotten the impression that the feeling was mutual. He liked her openness, honesty, and her ability to speak her feelings. He wanted to be able to do that, but he wasn't there. He didn't know if he would ever be able to do that. Was that even a part of the white knight?

He looked at the display for the knitters, and touched one of the skeins of yarn, it was baby-soft like Skye's hands. He took his hand away and looked around. He had it bad if he could think of her just by touching something soft. He wondered if her lips would be as soft; it didn't sound so far fetched.

He knew he didn't have the background to do this knight thing, but he knew how to do research. After work today he was going straight to the library, and he was going to research how to be a knight for Skye.

"You never schedule in the middle of the week," Lucy said as Skye laid down on the massage table. Lucy smiled at Skye and pulled back the heated blanket. "As you requested, I will be your masseuse for the day. We have an hour and a half with some sauna time scheduled. If I saw correctly, you're also here for a manicure and pedicure. Requesting me wasn't too much of a big thing, but for you to be here for the works, you've got to tell me, what gives?"

Skye had been friends with Lucy for about seven years. Lucy had come to visit Sweet Blooms with her estranged husband, and she hadn't left. Lucy had been so excited to open her spa. She wanted to create a city spa out in Sweet Blooms, and she had. People from other counties came to her spa, but she never expanded it; she kept it to its small size.

"I used my coupon, so don't get all loopy on me."

Lucy dimmed the lights and started the massage. "Are you going to tell me what's going on or do I have to wait until I get you to the sauna room?"

"No, you don't have to wait. I'll be singing while I'm on this table."

Lucy often joked that she was one-third masseuse,

one third marriage counselor, and one-third therapist.

"Confess away before I explode from not knowing," Lucy begged. "Whatever it is, it must be about a man because that's the only time a woman pulls out the works."

"It is about a man." Skye propped her head on her hands and looked at her friend from the side. "You'll need to keep this one under wraps until I figure it out. I need your worldly opinion," Skye started.

"Okay, go for it. I'm putting my city feelings on."

Now that the time was here, Skye was hesitating. Normally, she'd be talking about this with Hannah, but she didn't want to ruin Hannah's happiness with her doubts. She needed someone who had left Sweet Blooms. Someone who had a more worldly view than she did.

"Okay, here it is," Skye mumbled. "I think I found a guy I like."

"Okay."

"No, Lucy, I mean like in a prince charming kind of way. The feelings are strong. He's honest, and I'm instantly comfortable. It's probably helping a whole lot that Stephen liked him too."

Lucy already knew about the prince charming dream. She didn't think it was very practical. Lucy wasn't a proponent of being the damsel in distress and thought damsels should slay their own dragons.

"Then all should be great."

"The problem is, he's all wrong. He's not from here. He doesn't like people."

"Hold up. I may not be the brightest crayon in the bunch, but if he has all of these hangups, how can he be the one?"

"It's Caleb Mathews."

"Oh, well, I can see how all of those negatives wouldn't matter. That man is simply gorgeous in a brooding, caveman kind of way."

Skye grabbed the towel and turned to Lucy. "You've seen him?"

Lucy guided her back to the table.

"Skye, this is Sweet Blooms, and there's been a gorgeous man out running every morning through Sweet Blooms wearing tight pants that hug his thighs as he makes the rounds. Yes, I'm pretty sure everyone has seen Caleb, even if they don't know him by name."

"Well, it's not that he's attractive. I mean, it doesn't hurt, but that's not the focus. I know whenever I've talked about being with someone I always thought I would pick someone from in Sweet Blooms. You know, pick someone local, but then came Caleb," she said, letting out a long sigh. "So I guess the crux of it is, I'm going to try with Caleb. So I decided to go all out and get myself together. Do you think this is totally crazy?"

Lucy laughed and continued to do the massage.

"Well, let's address the issues one by one. You are not crazy, so we can take that off the table. Two, of all the men you could have chosen, Caleb might not have been my number one or two, but that's just because he seems really quiet and you, my friend, are not."

Skye laughed. "Yeah, I might have noticed."

Lucy let the silence hang between them, and she continued to do the massage. "At the end of the day, Skye, I think you should try to give you and Caleb a chance."

"I am. That's why I'm here. To get myself ready to give us both a chance."

"No, Skye. What I mean is you need to see how you and Caleb work out and not compare him to your parents. I didn't even meet them, and I have to tell you the image you paint of them seems almost unattainable."

Skye nodded and closed her eyes. It was hard to give up on the dream. So much had been taken. Her parents were gone. Stephen was gone. Now the things she had that seemed the closest to her were their memories.

Lucy broke into her thoughts. "I'm glad you were open to looking at Caleb. I mean, we're all open to looking at Caleb, but you know what I mean."

"Well, there hasn't been an influx of new guys my age in Sweet Blooms. I want to have a family, and I'd rather do it sooner than later," Skye confessed. "When I mentioned it to Caleb, he said he was going to mention it to me too, so—"

"Whoa there, little girl, what did you say?"

Skye thought on it and repeated. "He said he was going to mention it to me and—"

Lucy started laughing in the room. "I should have known. This is so you, Skye," she said between laughs.

Skye turned around to see Lucy sitting on a small circular chair wiping her eyes. "What?"

"Well, I thought you were saying you were going to try to attract this man. I had no idea you had already told him he's the one."

"Well, have you seen him? I didn't see the point in putting out clues. We live together, and we work together. So—"

Lucy waved her on. "Please, Skye, I'm the last one to give advice. You have a plan; let's see how it goes."

"Well, that's the other thing. I don't have a real plan.

Maybe I should make one and show him how to do it."

Lucy's smile just grew on her face. "Are you suggesting that you need to romance this man because he doesn't know how to romance you?"

Skye dropped her head into her hands. "Lucy, he had such a horrible childhood. I haven't heard him talk about any girlfriends or love interests. What happens if he doesn't know what to do?"

Lucy covered her mouth, stood up, and gestured for Skye to lay back down. "I know this is going to sound odd to you, but I think Caleb, who made it through the military and found you, will be able to figure out how to romance you. I mean, if he can't do this, it looks pretty dim for the other activities."

Skye yelped, and Lucy started giggling.

"Enough, Skye. Listen to me. How you start is how you end. Let him do this. Find out if he can be the man you need. Take today and relax, tomorrow will come soon enough."

Caleb thought he was a master at waiting. He was wrong. He had been waiting for Skye to come home, and the wait was worse than waiting for a target. It seemed like everyone in Sweet Blooms had dropped by. The Mayor had dropped by to make sure Skye was doing well. She didn't want to stay and seemed inordinately interested in where he was sleeping in the house.

A couple of other women stopped by to make sure Skye was okay as well. If he didn't know better, he'd think there had been a town bulletin that announced he was a suspected serial killer or, at the very least, a person of interest.

Caleb had been preparing the house and dinner for Skye. During lunch, he went to the library and read several books on how to be a contemporary white knight to the modern day woman. There was truly a book for everything. One book outlined a three, five, and seven-day plan to romance your modern day damsel. He got a little caught up on classifying her. The choice wasn't that clear to him either. According to the book, she was either Rapunzel—beautiful and unapproachable, Cinderella—hard working and independent, or Snow White—has money but always seems to be in trouble. He couldn't choose, so he looked at all of them and modified the plan to suit his needs and supplies.

He had gone out and purchased a couple of shirts and some jeans that weren't worn. It suggested he get some sunglasses, but he had his covers already. That was two hours ago. His meal was less than what it was supposed to be. Pasta didn't hold well, and he was about to go out and find her and bring her home when he saw her car coming up.

"You finally came home?" he grumbled as he walked out to meet her. Then he shook his head. This was not the greeting he had planned on. "Sorry, I made dinner."

The corners of her mouth lifted. "Not good at planning surprises?" she asked.

"I generally don't like surprises, but I read a book that says women love surprises. I think it ruins the continuity of the day, but that's what the consensus was."

"I like surprises," she murmured to Caleb.

He sighed. "Of course you do. Come on. I tried to make dinner. It's not what it should be, but it's edible."

"It's edible, huh? How do you know? Have you been eating it?" she teased.

"Well, the instructions said not to taste the food, but if you do to use a fresh spoon and saucer. I think it's clear whoever said that had a dishwasher or a maid to clean up all those dishes they were dirtying."

"I suppose they did." She looked at him, and he could see the laughter in her eyes. Caleb was confused. Was she laughing happy or was she laughing at him happy? It didn't make a difference at this point. She had come home, and he could get through this episode.

"Let's go inside and get comfortable," he said, offering his arm and walking her to the door.

Caleb held the door for her. When she walked in, he saw her take in the flowers in several vases placed throughout the room. She went to a vase of roses.

"These are beautiful, Caleb. You shouldn't have; these must have cost a fortune."

He looked around and nodded. "Not a fortune, but it put a dent in my expected monthly expenses."

She seemed like she was startled by that admission, and then she smiled.

"What's cooking?"

He led the way into her kitchen. He was frustrated, but he would make do. He asked her to sit down, and he went to serve up the pasta in white clam sauce. When he looked at it in the pot, it looked gelatinous. He looked over at her at the table smiling. While he put the pasta in a bowl, he remembered he was supposed to talk to her.

"So how was your day off?"

"Oh, it was great. I did some girl stuff that I had been neglecting."

He put the bowls into the microwave and looked at her. She looked like she was waiting for something. She must be hungry, he thought. The book had said to fill empty spaces with a conversation that showed he understood what she said.

"So you had to get shaved and waxed today?"

Skye choked, and Caleb immediately went to her side and gave her a healthy pound on the back in case she was choking.

"Stop! I'm fine now. I just swallowed wrong, thank you."

The microwave dinged, and he brought out the two steaming bowls of pasta and clam sauce. He set a bowl in front of Skye and then took a seat.

"It's older than when I made it, but it's still edible. Eat up."

He dug in and noticed the noodles were a bit mushy, and the clams were shriveled into chewy bites. It wasn't too bad though. It definitely beat other places he had eaten at. He looked up to see Skye, and she was looking at him, wide-eyed.

"Did you want me to get you something else to drink? I only drink water as a habit, but I purchased some other things because I wasn't sure what you drank."

She smiled and shook her head. "I'm good with water. Thank you."

Then he noticed she wasn't really eating. She was moving the noodles around more so than eating.

"You should eat up before it goes back to its gelatinous mass."

She gave him a smile. "I had some food at the spa before I came here, so I'm not so hungry." He looked into her eyes, and that was when he knew it.

"It's that bad, huh?"

She held up her hands. "No, no, it's just—"

Caleb sighed. "I know you're looking for the man of your dreams, and I get that. But I have a request to put in here. I need us to be honest with each other. Okay?"

Skye nodded.

"So the pasta was pretty bad?"

She squirmed, but finally, she nodded. "It was pretty bad."

Caleb got up and threw the plate away. He ignored Skye's protest.

"I'm sorry about that. Do you want anything else? We can go out or do something you would really like to do."

"No, I'm good. I wasn't really that hungry."

"That was kind of you to say that."

Skye chuckled. "Caleb, thank you. I didn't expect you to try so hard or so soon."

He sat down in the chair and reached out to the pitcher and poured them water.

"I didn't know what you drank, or if you drank wine at all, so I thought the water was safe."

She smiled and picked up the glass. "It's very safe."

Caleb reached across the table and put his hand on top of hers. "I'm trying here, Skye." He could feel her delicate pulse beneath his hands. Where his hands were scarred and beaten, Skye's hands were smooth and soft.

He hadn't realized he had been holding his breath until she placed her hand on top of his.

"This isn't supposed to be torture, Caleb."

"It's point of view, I suppose." He saw her pull back her hand and he felt the loss right away.

"What's wrong?" She asked.

Caleb shook his head. "It's nothing. This just takes some getting used to. I guess I didn't know how much of a bother this was."

"A bother?"

Caleb looked up to see Skye's stricken face. "I'm not saying you are a bother. I'm just saying this is a lot of effort, and then it doesn't work out right either. All of this inconsistency seems like something only a woman could love."

"So what are you saying, Caleb?"

"Don't get all wet and bristled. I'm just saying it's different. I'm not saying I won't do it. I'm just more of a straightforward kind of guy."

Skye sat back and gave him a guarded gaze. "Just what does that mean?"

"It means if you want to go out, I might suggest a burger joint. It means that flowers are okay once in a while. It means I'm a simple man. This took a mission plan in my head. We haven't even gone anywhere yet."

Skye had pushed herself away from the table. "I'm sorry it's a big to-do for you."

"Don't get upset. I just have to—"

"Caleb, why don't we stop talking about it while you're still ahead?" Both of them perked up when they heard a car coming into the driveway.

Caleb looked at Skye. "Are you expecting anyone?"

She shook her head no. They both went to the door and Skye opened it. A black 250 truck was in the driveway. Then a man—six foot one, lanky in an opened button-up long sleeve shirt—got out of the car. His sleeves were rolled up, and they showed he had some muscles under that shirt.

"Hello, I'm looking for Skye O'Malley?"

Skye brushed by Caleb without saying a word.

"I'm Skye, and you are?"

The man held out his hand and took an appraising look at Skye. Caleb moved closer so he could hear.

"I'm Pierce Morgan from the Cade's place. I was hoping to speak to you." He opened the door and brought out a single rose with a bottle of wine.

"I wasn't sure if you drank wine, but it seemed rude to come empty-handed."

It was in that moment that Caleb knew that Skye's knight in armor had shown up and his chances to get the girl were gone.

Seven

"Hello, Ms. O'Malley, the description I received didn't do you justice."

Skye raised her eyebrow as she listened to Pierce's voice.

"Mr. Morgan, how can I help you?"

Skye looked at his clothes and saw they were casually expensive. His shirt was tailored, and his pants fit him too well to be anything but tailored. The lack of dust on his shoes told her he was probably working in the off. All of this, topped off by the rose, had her betting the house he was some kind of salesman.

To his credit, he did have a head of black hair and smooth skin. Maybe he was in his late thirties, and he was a handsome man. As Lucy would say, there was just something off about him. How could she even say he was off, though, after that fiasco Caleb had tried to plan?

"I'm the new project manager at Adam Cade's place."

"Oh, well, welcome."

"I wish I could tell you that this was totally a social visit, but it isn't. I'm doing the work on the woodworking building Mr. Cade wants to construct.

I wanted to reach out to you as the local supplier to see if you had the raw items we need to build, or if you would be willing to be a drop-off place for the items?"

"We've never been asked before, but I don't see why not," she said.

Pierce pointed towards the house. "I can see the early architecture. Is that the original wood?"

Skye beamed. "Yes, it is. My mother was into restorations, and she saw this house and fell in love with it."

He pointed to Caleb. "I'm sorry, am I interrupting something?" he asked as Caleb moved to stand next to her.

"Caleb, this is Pierce. He's the project manager at the Cade ranch. He wanted to talk about business."

"We're eating dinner."

Skye laughed and took a step closer to Caleb, stepping on his foot. "Caleb is so funny. We were just finishing."

"No, I don't want to interfere. I can talk about business later," he said, heading towards his truck.

Skye gave Caleb a face and then called out to Pierce.

"Mr. Morgan, why don't we set up a time to meet. I can see this could be a good deal for both of us."

Pierce turned back to Skye and smiled. "I was hoping you would say that. I want to bring in some new people to get the work done."

Skye was a little confused. "New people? I thought Adam was using local talent."

Pierce's smile tightened. "Actually, Adam left it to me to get the task done the most efficiently. That being the case, I'll be using my own resources."

"Oh, I see," Skye said. Actually, she didn't understand this change at all as Pierce drove away.

Eight

If Pierce had ever been to a store, it wasn't apparent when he walked into Skye's the next morning. Skye knew who he was right away. He was dressed in another casual corporate outfit, walking up and down the aisles looking at the displays. Skye supposed that was the norm where he was from.

Every now and again Pierce would bump into a person as he perused her aisles. She wondered how big of a change it was for him. Certainly, if his ride was any indication of what he was expecting, hers must seem to be the poor man's supply shop.

"I wonder if he's really going to use our store?" Cassandra asked Skye.

Skye gave Pierce another once over, then smiled. In his hand, he had another gift. She presumed it was for her. "I don't know if he's doing business with the store, but he's trying to do something with me," she whispered.

"Are you looking for someone? I thought you were with Caleb?"

Skye thought about the disaster of the dinner. "I don't know if Caleb really wants to do anything with me.

I think he's of the mindset that I might be too much of a bother."

Cassandra touched Skye's shoulder. "Men are fickle, but Caleb seems pretty steady. Maybe you two just got off to a bad start?"

Skye looked at Cassandra and gave it some thought. "Maybe, but I can't focus on that now. Let's see what Mr. Morgan can do for the store, if anything."

She walked out into the aisle and watched him look over some blankets that were in the store on consignment. "Can I help you, Mr. Morgan?"

Pierce turned around and smiled at her. "Call me Pierce, please, and I bring gifts," he said, holding out a bakery box with a cupcake inside.

Skye took the box and nodded to him. "Thank you. Please don't feel obligated to give me gifts. I assure you all of the business decisions are based on business."

Pierce straightened up and smiled. "I didn't mean to imply otherwise."

"Please, tell me why you came by."

"I came by to continue the discussion from yesterday. I have some guys coming in from the city, and they need to store the lumber in a dry place."

"It depends on how much lumber you have. I can ask Robert; he does that kind of work as well, you know storing supplies if people need them space, so I know if I can't accommodate the space, he'll help us out."

"That's great. Since you already have all of the connections in town, I think it would be easier if I could go over my plans with you. Would you like to go to dinner?"

Before Skye could answer, a woman's voice in distress filled the store. Skye followed the sound to aisle three where there were glass figurines—some on shelves and some shattered on the floor—and one horrified mother of two very regretful-looking boys.

The mother had set her children on the side while she tried to fix the mess.

"I'm so sorry. They didn't mean to do it," the woman said frantically.

Skye looked at the woman and her kids. The children were clean, but their clothes had seen better days, and the mother looked worn and more depressed by the moment.

"Hello, let me do that," Skye said. She moved the woman to the side, but Robert was already there cleaning up the glass.

"I—I'm so sorry. I don't know what it costs, but I can see what I can do."

Skye placed her hand on the young mother's arm. "It's no problem. These things happen." Skye then turned to the boys who looked as if they were going to cry.

"Hi fellas, are you okay?"

Both of the boys looked to their mother before answering. They were at best five-year-olds.

"We're sorry. It wouldn't let go of our hands."

Both of the boys nodded to affirm the story. They held up their hands, and Skye could see the sticky red sugar candy on their hands.

"I can see how it wouldn't let go. I think you should go to your mother and let her clean you up before you have this problem again."

The mother smiled at Skye and ushered her children towards the store entrance. When she stood up, Pierce was there.

"That was very kind. Will you let me pay for the merchandise?"

"No, it's no worry. I have insurance for these kinds of things," she replied.

"Then let me take you to the coffee house. I saw one around the corner. We can sit there for a moment."

Skye hesitated, not sure if she should go with Pierce. It was odd, but she felt a little guilty. When she stood up and looked around the store, Caleb wasn't there. He was in the back doing inventory. Then she looked at Pierce, and he was there with an arm out, waiting for her just like her dad had done for her mom. It wasn't like she was getting engaged; it was just coffee. "Thank you, I'd love to."

They walked down the block. He held the door open for her and then pulled out a chair for her. When it was time to order, he took her order, and when the waitress came, he gave it to the waitress. Once she was gone, and they were waiting for their coffee and snack, Pierce smiled at her. "I noticed there seem to be a lot of female-owned businesses in town."

Skye smiled. "Sweet Blooms is full of entrepreneurial women. It happens that the guys go away to make their fortune and then come home. The girls tend to stay in town, or other women come into town and find Sweet Blooms is a great place to raise a family."

"Do you have family here?"

Skye's smile dimmed. Pierce reached out and touched her hand. "I'm sorry to intrude. You don't have to answer."

Skye shook her head. "No, no, it's fine. I'm the only one left in my family."

"It must be lonely in such a family-orientated town."

"It can be."

Pierce cleared his throat, and the waitress brought their order to the table. "I feel a bit lost here as well. I'm from the city, and there's usually a single's place, but not here."

Skye laughed. "We don't usually do singles places. Unless you're going to be around on Sunday, because the first three rows of the church are usually for singles. We're not so far off from the city, you can commute on the weekends."

"I could, but I want to give my best to this project."

"A good work ethic is appreciated in Sweet Blooms."

"I wanted to make sure it wasn't too much of an inconvenience to store the lumber with you."

"No, we'll take care of that for you."

"I'll probably have some other vendors coming as well, but I'll let you know."

Skye thought the request was a bit odd. "Why don't you want to use the storage on the Cade site?"

Pierce smiled and answered, "The buildings are being rebuilt, not all of them are ready to hold supplies. Until they clear them of vermin and dry rot, I don't want to put fresh supplies there."

"Okay."

Pierce leaned towards her. "Thank you so much for helping me and taking the time to talk to a stranger."

"It's no problem, and please don't think of yourself as a stranger. You can come over anytime."

Pierce called for the check. When it came, he promptly paid for it before Skye could even reach for it.

"Again, I want to thank you for taking the time."

"No, really, it was no bother. And next time I'll pay the check."

"I look forward to it," he said with a smile. He walked her back to the storefront and then went on his way.

It was the end of the day, and Skye had sent everyone home. Cassandra stayed to put up the sale signs and restock the shelves for the special orders in the morning. Skye was in the back room going over the inventory Caleb had done earlier. The man had impeccable handwriting. He had not only taken inventory, but he'd organized the shelves to match the paper. She was almost done adding up the value in stock and storage when Cassandra showed up in the doorway.

Cassandra stood in the doorway to the front of the store. She had a grin on her face a mile wide. "You have a visitor."

Skye was on alert. Maybe it was Pierce? She hadn't expected him to come back so soon. "Pierce?"

"Nope, try again." Cassandra stepped aside.

Skye looked behind her and saw Caleb there with a picnic basket. She knew he had heard her say, Pierce. When she caught his eye, he moved forward into the room.

It was the confidence that came with him that always struck her. Pierce might be polite, but there was something innate to Caleb that just made her tingle. It wasn't just his face or his body, although both were impressive. If there were a picture next to the definition of *man* in the dictionary, it would have been a picture of Caleb.

"Hi," he said as he set the picnic basket on the table. "I had hoped we could do lunch, but this time I planned ahead and had someone make us dinner. Are you hungry?"

Skye nodded. "I thought you were going back to the house."

"No, I wanted us to try take two to dinner. I might even have the hang of it now," he said with a smile.

She cleared the table and watched him as he unpacked the basket and set up the table. "Sometimes the second time is the charm." She peeked around him. "Did Cassandra leave?"

"Yes, she was trying to be discreet, but she left out the front," he said, taking a breath. "I think if there's good news and bad news, we should always address the bad news. It was one of the things Stephen and I agreed on."

Skye nodded and smiled. "He did say that. His thought was if we take care of the bad news first, then we can languish over the good news, and that would be the last thing on everyone's mind. So yes, I totally agree. Although I don't see how that is relevant here?"

"Pierce." Before she could speak, he held up his hand. "Give me a moment, and we'll go on." Skye nodded.

"I don't like him. He's sneaky."

Skye smiled. "You got that from?"

"He's too clean."

Skye had to stop the laugh from coming out of her mouth. "Let me see if I understand correctly. You haven't spoken to the man, and you haven't heard him speak. You are making your judgment on him because he has good hygiene?"

Caleb shrugged. "It's beyond good hygiene. As dusty as it is out here, he never has a speck of dirt on him. A person that clean has to put effort into it. If he puts that much effort into it, he's hiding something. He's sneaky."

Skye grinned. "Well, I have no answer to that. I will keep it in mind, though. Are we done?"

Caleb nodded. "Yup. I'm good. I warned you."

Skye shook her head and waited. Caleb looked at her, and a moment went by before he seemd to have an epiphany.

"Oh! I'm serving," Caleb said.

"Caleb, you're too much sometimes."

"I can't imagine what you're talking about. What you see is what you get with me."

"Really? Is anybody really like that?"

Caleb shrugged as he made sure all the Tupperware containers were open and within reach. "Some of us don't have a choice. I can't be bothered enough to lie."

She started serving out pieces of chicken and salad to both of their plates while he made sure the silverware and napkins were handy. "Are you trying to tell me you have never told a lie?"

"Not successfully. Anyway, I wanted to talk about this afternoon."

Skye looked warily at him. "I thought we already talked about Pierce?"

Caleb waved that away. "No, I'm not talking about Pierce, at least not directly. What happened this afternoon is you went off with Pierce because you didn't know I wanted to have lunch with you. We can fix that from ever happening again."

Skye looked confused. "Stop me from seeing Pierce again?"

"No, not that. That will happen on its own when you find out he's slimy. What I'm talking about is a schedule."

"I'm sorry?"

"No commander goes into battle without a plan. No team goes in without a schedule and checkpoints. I think while we are trying this relationship thing, we need a schedule," he said. "This way you'll know when I'm coming, and I'll know you are going to be in a place so I can plan a surprise."

She finished the bite of chicken in her mouth. "Caleb, how can it be a surprise if it's scheduled?"

"Because you don't know the details."

Skye could see that it was a complete answer for him, so she shook her head and told him to carry on. "Okay, let's compromise. You make a schedule and let me know the day of. I don't think I really want to know the schedule."

Caleb cocked his head to the side and looked at her. "You don't want to know the schedule?"

Skye smiled at his confused face. "Nope!"

They finished the meal with lots of small talk, and Skye could see that Caleb was on his very best behavior. After the meal, he packed it all up and told her to wait at the store, and they'd go home together.

After such a pleasant meal, she decided to tease him. "You just want me to stay around so you can get a ride. Is Caleb afraid of the dark?"

Caleb stood in front of her and moved closer until they were forehead to forehead. "No, Ms. Skye, I don't need a ride home. I'm going to make sure you get to your front door safely. I'm not afraid of the dark. The dark is usually afraid of me. I'll be back."

She watched him leave, and the thought wouldn't leave her—that man could work a room and not move a muscle. When he did move, it was grace, beauty, and desire working in tandem. She was supposed to be focusing on his character and not his physique.

Nine

Caleb waited for Skye outside the store. He had his truck today, and he had left her a note that they were going to meet and he was going to take them someplace. When he wanted to explain the details, she waved him off. Personally, Caleb didn't get the whole *it's a surprise* thing, but it was what she wanted, so here they were.

He'd picked up some macarons from the coffee shop. Cassandra had told him that macarons were Skye's guilty pleasure. He'd been reading more books on white knight syndrome and decided she didn't really want that kind of man. A man like that didn't really fit her personality. So tonight he was going to go with the idea of sharing something with her that he liked to do, and it was also something he and Stephen had done every so often. The macaroons were the bribe to make sure she got in the car.

As usual, she was the last one out of the building. She didn't know, but he waited for her every night. When she drove home, he would take the five-mile jog to the house. It was a good jog, and it made him feel better knowing she was okay.

He saw her coming out of the store, and she looked a little droopy. He started to rethink tonight's activity but ultimately decided to go with his initial plan. If it all went well, she would have a great adrenaline rush and feel better. Even he had to admit today had been a beast. The tourists were starting to flood into Sweet Blooms. It was great for business, but trying to keep the shelves stocked and talk to the customers was tiring.

He waved, and she started walking towards him. When he saw her he watched—and definitely appreciated—her curves as she moved across the street. However, he also saw the way she looked at everyone around her, even the old lady who was walking between her and Caleb, and she smiled at them all. She called one or two out by name.

That was Skye. She was humble and kind. She had no artifice, and she was the type of woman that gave a jaded man like Caleb something to believe in.

"You brought your truck?" she said. "I've already got mine. Tell me where we're going, and I'll follow."

"One, where we are going is a surprise. Two, I realize you brought your vehicle, but I'm hoping the lure of French macarons will get you to trust your car to the store for one night."

Skye smiled. "I don't know who you asked, but whoever it was, tell them score for me. I will certainly follow sugar."

She got into the truck, and he drove for about twenty minutes.

"Caleb?"

He could hear the question in her voice. "We're almost there." About ten minutes later he stopped the truck. "We're here."

Skye looked out of the window. "We're nowhere." Off to the side of the road, Caleb walked towards his firepit. He touched the stones that lay at the bottom, making sure they were still hot. Then he reached down and picked up a backpack. He turned and gave it to Skye.

"Are we camping?"

Caleb smiled. "We're camping after. First I want us to share something that helped Stephen and me at the end of the day."

She took the backpack and looked inside. "You have got to be kidding me."

Caleb smiled and shook his head no. "I'm totally not kidding you."

She pulled out the running outfit and the matching socks and shoes.

"The heat is still on in the truck. You can change in there if you want."

Skye looked at Caleb with an *I don't get it* look. "You really expect me to run with you?"

Caleb shook his head no. "I expect that the two of us will run, and when you are tired, we will turn back to the camp."

"And then we'll drive to the perfectly functioning house?"

"No, then we will follow up the run with sleeping in the great outdoors. Stephen always thought if you tried this you would love it."

Skye clutched the bag closer to her chest. She grumbled, "I'll be back."

When she emerged from the car in the clothes he'd gotten her, Caleb could tell he had picked the right sizes. He would never look at workout wear the same.

He knew Skye was a woman with a great shape, but these workout clothes fit her like a second skin. With every move she made, he could see every muscle group.

Pulling her hair back into a ponytail, she rubbed her arms and tapped her foot on the ground. "I'm cold."

Caleb smiled. "You know when I hear that, what I really hear is you need to heat up."

Skye smiled. "You're right. Let's get to the car and turn on the heat."

He walked over to her and put his hands on her shoulders. "I completely agree with you. Let's go ahead and do some walking first though."

Skye looked at him skeptically. "Okay."

Caleb nodded. "After we stretch for a bit."

Skye followed along, and ten minutes later they were running on trails she knew but ones that she normally would be walking. At first, she was focusing on the run, and then as she fell into a pace, she focused on Caleb.

"Are we done yet?"

Caleb turned around, running backward. "We just started. Are you feeling warm yet?"

"I'm dying. Is this your idea of romantic?" she yelled at him. She stopped running and stood with her hands on her hips. "I'm done!"

He went to stand in front of her, still jogging in place. "Okay, we're at the place we need to be anyway."

Skye looked confused. "Wh-what are you talking about?" she said through gasping breath. "There's nothing here."

Caleb stopped running and pointed up. Skye followed where he was pointing up into a tree. In the tree there looked to be a ledge of some sort. Caleb walked to the tree and pulled out a rope.

"Can you climb, Skye? Or do you need me to carry you up?"

She looked at him indignantly. Pushing back her hair, she grabbed the rope and fingered the knots in it. "Of course I can climb." Without giving him another glance, she began to climb up.

He watched her tackle the rope. Her determination was one of the many attractive things about her. He heard her grunting, but not once did she ask for help. "You okay, country girl?"

She stopped and looked below. She had a devilish smile on her face. "I know why you sent me up, army boy. You wanted me to make sure all was clear. It's okay, I won't tell anyone," she said with a laugh.

She continued to climb the last three knots. Caleb pulled himself up and was at the top just as she was clearing the rope.

"I needed you to make sure all was well, huh?" he said, laughing. Skye wasn't laughing. Instead, she was looking at the flat he had built. He had put five planks on the tree and covered it in a cloth cover. Then he had brought several bowls and filled them with desserts and flowers.

"I didn't know which ones you liked, so I got an assortment of desserts and flowers for you. There are two thermoses over there as well. One has tea, and one has coffee. I took into account it might be nippy tonight."

Skye looked at him and blinked, holding back tears.

"How did you know?"

Caleb smiled. "Stephen told me you two used to have a treehouse but the wood rotted and no one ever built a new treehouse. He said you told each other your secrets and made promises that only you two knew."

Skye walked gingerly over to the bowls, peering in

each one. Finally, she settled on one and picked up a thermos, sitting cross-legged in the middle of the platform. She held out a hand. "Come join me. Or is this so unsteady that you think you'll fall?"

Caleb put his hand to his chest. "I'm shocked that you would think I, of all people, don't know how to build a sturdy platform."

He grabbed the other thermos and sat down. Both of them ate in silence before she spoke.

"I don't think I can do this," she whispered.

"Do what exactly? Have dessert and tea in a treehouse? Well, not a treehouse but a tree porch?"

Skye smiled. "No. The *try a relationship* thing." She wouldn't look at him, so he reached out and tilted her chin up towards him.

"Look a guy in the eye when you want to let him down. Can you tell me why?"

"I think you're so different and I may not be ready for that."

"Ah, it's the famous, *it's not you, it's me* conversation."

Skye turned away from him and looked at the landing. "This is too foreign. It's too different. What happens if it's exciting now, but I can't compete with this."

He listened to her try and find some leg of logic to grab onto.

"You're going to have to throw me a better line than that, Skye. Is it that you prefer the clean guys like Pierce? Do I not make the cut for your friends?"

She took a deep breath and let out a moan of confusion. "Caleb, you seem so sure of who you are, and you've been around the world and seen other places and other women. I won't measure up at all."

Caleb let out a sigh and smiled. "You think there's a

woman who could compare to you? If I had met her, I wouldn't be here."

Skye looked at him and swallowed. "I don't think that's how it works."

"Oh yes, that's how it works for me. If I had met a woman who could make me think about staying in one place, I would have tried it, but I didn't. Are you worried that I'll compare you to any other woman I've had in my life?"

He could see her eyes getting larger and larger. Those eyes were wide open and innocent. In them, he saw hope, beauty, and unconditional love he didn't even know existed.

"I'm scared, Caleb."

"Guess what, Skye, I'm scared too. I'm scared you'll look at me and see a washed up army guy who's only worthwhile attribute is killing. I'm scared that you'll wake up one day and say, 'I'm good with Stephen's passing, and I don't really need that canker sore of a vet anymore.' Or even worse, I'm scared that one day that glow of love and goodness will be dimmed because you're stuck with me."

Skye smiled. "Don't worry about any of those things. You're a great package, and there's good in you, Caleb. It's just raw. Me, I've been waiting for a fairy tale."

Caleb reached out and ran his hand over her soft cheek. Touching her grounded him in ways he didn't know he was missing. "It's fitting that a princess would be waiting on a fairytale."

"You make me feel special, Caleb."

He took a napkin and wiped some crumbs from her face. "I don't make you feel this way. You are the way you are."

He saw a tear on her cheek before she wiped it away. "Do you think these treats will get you anywhere with me?"

Caleb laughed. "I sure hope so, because they were expensive."

She laughed. "Then I guess we better eat them."

After they had finished eating and drinking tea, they both walked back to the car.

"So I noticed you have a lot of rules," Skye said.

"Really?" Caleb replied. Skye looked at him and smiled. He seemed so shocked by her statement.

"I'm not a fan of rules. In fact, I like to find ways around them," she said, laughing when his eyebrows went up.

"Rules kept me alive, but for you, I'll entertain the notion that breaking a rule or two might not be so bad."

"Really? Like what?" Skye teased, liking this new side of Caleb.

He walked over to the truck and leaned against it, then held out his hand.

"I don't kiss on the first date or the second, but since this turned out really well, I'll make an exception."

She looked at his hand, and that feeling was back. It started as a little heat in her stomach, grew into a gathering of butterflies, and then spread like brush fire until she was taking deep breaths to keep cool. With each step she took towards him, her breath came faster. Her body didn't know if she should run to him or from him. When there was a foot between them, she stopped.

"Well, that's a politically correct distance to be from me," he said.

Wariness and curiosity warred within her. It was Caleb, but this was a different Caleb. She wanted to get closer to know what would happen. To get to know Caleb in a personal way. She licked her lips and stepped into his personal space.

He held up his hands on both sides and put them behind his back.

"I'm asking you to trust me. I want to make sure I keep that trust."

"So you're putting your hands behind your back?" she asked.

"I'm making sure I can trust me. So I'm going to kiss you. You get to decide when we're done."

Skye's eyes were wide, and her heartbeat was pounding so hard in her chest that she was sure Caleb could hear it. This wasn't like a fairytale. Prince Charming wasn't going to sweep her off of her feet. Instead, Prince Charming was asking her to give him a kiss. Part of her wanted to know what it would be like to give a man like Caleb a kiss. The other part of her just wanted to run. Wanted to run from the new situation and run from the change in roles.

"Okay," she said in a wobbly voice.

She had hoped he would smile or do something that would encourage her to kiss him. He did nothing but wait. Her chest got tight, and the butterflies had coagulated into a heat that was unbearable. She leaned in and brushed her mouth over his.

His lips didn't move, and she pulled away.

"If you don't want to kiss me, you could just tell me," she tossed the words at him.

Caleb licked his lips and held her gaze. "You didn't kiss me. Even on its best days, that was a peck. Come on, princess. I'm not moving. You get to call the shots."

She took a deep breath and leaned closer to Caleb. Her hands rested on his shoulders. The heat from his body ran like a current through hers. She closed her eyes and reveled in it. When she opened her eyes, he was looking straight at her.

She leaned in and placed a kiss on one side of his neck and then on the other. With each kiss, she had more confidence. Finally, she kissed the side of his mouth and then the other. Taking a deep breath, she leaned in, parted her lips, and brushed her mouth over his until his lips started to move under hers. She relaxed against him a little more, letting the pleasure of the moment move through her. Finally, she pulled away.

"Are you done, princess?" he asked in a low voice.

"I'm done," she whispered.

"Hop in and let's go home."

"I thought we were—"

Caleb had a wobbly smile. "I think we've broken enough rules for today."

Caleb drove them to the house and then cut the engine to his truck. Skye waited. She didn't know if there was something more. Nothing was going the way she had anticipated. She had no regrets, but she also didn't know what to do next.

"You're thinking so loud. I can hear you."

Skye laughed nervously.

"Listen, princess, we're done for the night. I have to do something with the truck. Tonight you gave the kiss; next time, I will."

Skye nodded and went into the house. She didn't bother to turn on the lights and just got ready for bed. She thought about Caleb and the kiss when she got into bed and carried the memory into her dreams.

Ten

Caleb was helping Robert during lunch to load the supplies into the truck and take them to Robert's storage barn on his property. Caleb could tell something was bothering Robert, but he didn't want to pry.

When they both got into the truck to make the last haul to his place, he didn't turn on the radio like he had done on the other trips. Caleb had decided he was going to intervene. He blamed his sudden thought to intervene on Skye. After last night and letting her take the lead, he started to give some thought to being around people. Not for his sake, but he knew Skye was more social than he would ever be. Last night had been a test of his resolve. He didn't realize how the kiss would draw him in and how hard it would be not to pull her into his arms. Only she could make him not being in control an addictive feeling.

Robert gave him a look and started up the truck. Robert's place was a good forty minutes away. Robert hadn't offered any information about who lived out on his place, but there were some rumors he had heard that Robert gave passing vets a place to stay if they needed it.

"Robert, I want to stick my nose somewhere you didn't ask," Caleb said as they went down the main road that led out of downtown proper to the farms.

"You can ask. It don't mean I'll answer, but I'll hear the question," Robert told him.

"You've been a little distant while we've been moving the supplies," Caleb started.

"When you ask a question, I'll answer," Robert replied.

"What I'm asking is, what's the problem? I would think you're getting a little bit of money from this, and so is Skye, but you look and act like it's the end of the world."

Robert was silent for a moment, as if thinking, and then nodded. "It's true. I'm making a little bit of money on this. The problem is I don't think I want money that comes this way."

"I don't get it," Caleb said.

"These supplies are coming from outside vendors."

"Yeah, I understand that Pierce is from the city, so all of his contacts are there. It figures that he would use the people he knows."

"I know one of the conditions was to use local help. That was part of getting the classes and setting up the woodshop. It would be homegrown, and home built."

"Have you talked to Adam?"

Robert shook his head. "It seems like everything is working okay, so I'm not sticking my nose in it. I was content to do so, but there are some things that are just bothering me."

"Everyone respects your opinion. I think if you bring it up, that will at least let everyone confirm or reply to the current goings-on."

Robert nodded. A few more moments of silence passed before Robert broke the silence.

"I have a gut question for you, Caleb."

"Shoot."

"What do you think about Pierce Morgan?"

Caleb sucked in his breath. "That's a hard one for me. I want to say that I've never liked the man because we've been looking at the same woman but—"

"But what?"

"I never really liked him at all. He's too clean."

Robert nodded. "I get you."

Caleb shifted in his chair a bit to stretch out in the passenger seat. "What exactly does Pierce do?"

"He's supposed to be their project manager. He gives the directions on how they're building, he's supposed to keep the reserves to a minimum, and to keep cost low. I think that's one of the reasons using Sweet Blooms' resources was supposed to be a given. We can move supplies and other items between people on their farms and in town. I'm not liking what I see."

"Did I hear Cassandra correctly when she said that you used to do this kind of work?"

Robert nodded. "I was born in Sweet Blooms, and I was in construction for a while. Then I went to the service, and then came back to Sweet Blooms. They say home is where the heart is, so I came back."

"Well, I can tell it's starting to bother you."

Robert shrugged and let out a breath. "I think the thing that's starting to bother me is that some of the materials aren't the right quality and treatment to build the woodworking house. I don't want to intrude with Adam because I know he's good at woodworking, but I don't think he's looking it over. So now I think this Pierce guy is sourcing from outside of Sweet Blooms and the materials are questionable."

"It's not like you to hesitate on what you have to say."

Robert let out a sigh. "The real issue is the family. You see, the girl I was in love with is Adam's grandmother. I don't know how it go if I went and told him that I think his business manager isn't doing the job the right way or the way he was approved by the board."

"Yeah, I can see the problem with that. What are the chances that you're wrong?"

Robert laughed. "Boy, you've been hanging around Skye too long. The chances that I'm wrong are slim to none."

Caleb laughed too. "You're right. I am hanging around Skye more. I've also learned from her that people who think they're always right have a skewed sense of right usually."

Robert smiled. "Yep, that's the first sign of getting into a relationship."

Caleb laughed. "Tell me."

"Things that made sense before now don't. A week ago you were right most of the time. Now you're in love's glow, and no one can be right all the time because she said so. Oh, how the mighty have fallen."

Caleb laughed. "Maybe. But it's a great fall. Seriously, I think you should talk to Pierce. Maybe he can provide some light on this."

Robert grunted. "Maybe I'll do that."

Pierce supposed at some time or another he would have to come out to the place where the supplies were kept. He didn't anticipate it would be so soon in the project, but that was the price for working in a small town. He looked at the road and thought about how much being in this town had cost him in dry cleaning alone. He knew that Adam was a millionaire and that doing business with him now would be good currency for the future.

Pierce thought Adam was like all the other millionaire rich boys that he knew. At some point or another, they all said they wanted to retreat from the city and move into an out of the way area. To date, he didn't know one of them that had actually managed to stay out of the city. He knew Adam Cade would be no different.

"You have to pay your dues with the little people," he murmured as he closed his door softly. He didn't want to slam it and kick up any dust into his interior.

Pierce didn't understand why people liked ranches, and he definitely wasn't thrilled to be here. He thought about saying no, but when he found out that the grungy old security guard was the person that Skye had sourced the supplies from, he figured he needed to take a look at the old man and make sure he wasn't a problem.

"Morgan."

He turned and saw Robert coming towards him, followed by two dogs. As the dogs came closer, Pierce could see they had no leashes.

"Are the dogs tamed?"

Robert looked at both dogs and made a hand gesture, and both dogs sat down.

"They are as tame as anything that still has its own will and its own teeth," Robert replied. "Follow me, and we can get out of the sun."

It was the first sensible thing the man had said. Pierce waited for the dogs to pass. These dogs weren't the kinds he was used to. His friends had miniature schnauzers and Shih Tzus. Those dogs were small and attractive. These dogs were large and looked like they could eat those smaller dogs in a pinch.

Yesterday, he had gotten a call from one of his suppliers that Robert had called to tell them there was a quality control issue with some of the wood. Needless to say, the vendor was less than pleased and called Pierce up right away. Pierce didn't want to recall that whole conversation, but the gist of it was for him to get his small town connections in line.

Robert led Pierce into a house that was functional, and that was being gracious. The furniture was stuffed and had checkerboard or floral print on it. The floor was covered in occasional throw rugs that didn't seem to have any rhyme or reason. The walls were filled with pictures. There were color pictures and black and white pictures in frames of all types. Pierce could tell a few of the frames were store-bought, but a lot of them were hand made.

"I've got some coffee on," Robert said, taking a seat at his kitchen table. When Pierce took a seat as well, he could see the kitchen table was really just a square folding table that a person would be more likely to play poker at than to have a real meal on.

Pierce tried to size up Robert. After all, that was his job—to find the weak points of a person and use it to his advantage. Pierce could tell that Robert didn't care about money or looks simply by looking around him at his home. He did see a group shot of a military unit in one of the homemade frames, so he was patriotic. The idiosyncrasy was that Robert's clothes all looked custom made.

"I didn't expect you to come out here," Robert said.

Pierce was saying the same thing to himself as well.

"This is one of the few times that I've been in a small town doing such a big project. I wanted to make sure I knew where the supplies were and, if possible, to check on them to make sure all is well, and that the deliveries are going as planned."

Robert nodded and took a sip of his coffee.

Pierce was offended. Robert had gotten coffee but hadn't poured him any. In fact, it appeared that when Robert offered coffee, he really meant for Pierce to get it himself. This was just one more reason he had to move this along.

"I got a call from one of my vendors. They said you called them and had a question about the quality of the supplies. I wanted to make sure I touched base with you to make sure you were satisfied with the shipment."

Pierce waited, hoping that the Achilles heel for Robert was being acknowledged as doing his job really well and being a part of the team. Then, after a few moments, something happened that Pierce had never experienced. Robert laughed.

Pierce smiled and then shook his head in confusion. "Did I say something funny?"

Robert took another sip of his coffee and was still grinning. "How often do those games work on other people?" Robert asked.

"Excuse me?" Pierce asked.

"I think we should start out straight from the beginning," Robert said.

Pierce nodded, making sure he had his concerned face on. Inside he was thinking *no, please, not another good old boy who wants us to be friends.*

"I know you are aware of the crappy quality of the supplies."

"Really, I wanted to discuss—"

Robert held up his hand. "Let me finish before you start weaving. All of these supplies are coming from places you normally do business with. I'm even going to venture that you do a lot of business with them. I can get that from the way they called you so quickly to say you might have a problem."

"Really, Robert, I don't know where you get these ideas."

"You don't have to admit or deny anything. Even if the quality of the supplies were okay, the other issue is why you didn't get the lumber from town. Part of the agreement for the building was you would use local resources."

"What are you, the town council police?" Pierce snapped. "I use administrative help from the town. It doesn't state all of it must come from this town."

"You're right, but the understanding isn't what you're doing."

Pierce stood up and brushed his pants off.

"Listen, I think you are very diligent to look out for the town resources and to look into how things are being done, but Adam Cade is a businessman, and he entrusted me to run this project. I have to use the resources that I think are best. And I have. So, while I appreciate your diligence, I'm going to have to ask you to let me do my job. Also, I'll look into moving the supplies someplace else. Good day."

With that, Pierce took two steps to the door and heard two low growls. It froze him in his tracks. Pierce turned slowly to see both dogs standing and tense. He looked to Robert who was still drinking his coffee.

"You see, Mr. Morgan, we're not the city. We keep our word. We treat others fairly. I'm not seeing any of those characteristics in you. I know you may think you've got this, but I'm telling you. You need to use more local resources. Power and perceptions can be confusing. I'm thinking you think you had the power when you came over. Now look, you can't even leave the room. Don't let your perceived power and authority go to your head."

With his speech made, Robert made a hand gesture, and both dogs sat down, looking at their master with tongues out.

"Thank you for the lesson." Pierce walked out of the house and back to his car. He had to find a new place to store his goods because he could see Robert was going to be a problem.

"You're really an outdoorsy person," Skye said as she followed Caleb. He had driven them outside again and, thank goodness, no running was required.

"As nature loving as you are, that's actually the last thing I expected to hear you say," he said with laughter in his voice.

"I love nature, but you have to admit you usually take it to a whole new level," she said sarcastically.

"This was on the schedule that you didn't want to have. Which, I want you to know, you can change your mind about at any time and receive a schedule within the hour."

"No thanks. Besides, it was so hot today. I'll take the chance with you just to get out," she confessed.

Caleb had met her for breakfast and told her today was a "them" day. She should be ready by noon. She was excited and cautious at the same time but she couldn't really credit why. She was more comfortable with Caleb, but he was still unpredictable. She hoped they weren't building the treehouse today. The fact that it wasn't out of the question was what gave her that little extra bit of nervousness.

She couldn't even think about that kiss without turning red, and that was when she was alone.

They walked into a clearing and then she knew where she was. In front of her was a sparkling lake. She and Stephen had come to this lake so many times. It was their hideaway. Actually, everyone knew where it was, but it was a bit of a walk, so if you didn't have a car it wasn't really feasible to do. When she was in front of the lake, she closed her eyes and let the memories come.

She remembered Stephen teaching her how to swim here and running here when their parents had passed away. She was here with Stephen before he was deployed, the memory was bittersweet in heart. It wasn't the deep open wound to her soul anymore and she could think about her twin and remember the good times.

"Hey? Is this too much or a bad idea? We can come back, or not; tell me what you want to do," Caleb said.

This man constantly surprised her. How could she explain to him the gifts he gave her?

"No, I'm actually okay."

Caleb smiled. "Good. There are some bushes around. I brought your bathing suit, you can change into it, and I'll do the same."

Skye was confused. "You brought my bathing suit? I didn't buy a suit this year or last, so what do you have and how did you get it?" she asked suspiciously.

Holding his hands in front of him in defense, he started talking. "Hold up. Before you get it in your head that I'm riffling through your personals while you aren't there, let me confess. I asked Lucy the spa lady to get it. I assumed she got it from you."

Now Skye was really curious.

"Well, hand it over. You've got my curiosity up."

He handed her the bag. She opened it and saw a beautiful one-piece with a tropical scene on it.

"It's gorgeous," she whispered.

"I thought so too, so I didn't question it."

Skye shrugged. "Okay, let's change. I'm dying to see your swimwear."

Caleb snorted. "It's not swimwear. I have trunks. No speedos, and nothing tight; just plain old trunks," he grumbled as he went to the bushes.

When both came out a few moments later, he nodded in appreciation.

"You clean up pretty good, Skye."

She waved him off. "Whatever."

Caleb laughed and then went to his gym bag. "What's in the bag?" she asked.

Caleb stood up. "First, I want you to notice I brought two bags—there is one on your side, and this one is mine."

"Okay," she said, still confused. "But what's in them?"

Caleb reached in and pulled out a water gun and a water balloon. Skye looked at him and started laughing.

"What?"

She managed to pull herself together and reply. "You look so funny with that neon yellow and orange water gun and red water balloons. It's like cartoon Rambo."

Caleb smiled. "You are the first to ever tell me that, and I have a reply."

Caleb threw the water balloon at her and hit her right in the stomach. The balloon didn't hurt, but the sudden splash of water made her suck in her breath. The sun was high though, and the chill went away to be replaced by the need to play.

"Are you sure you want to go down this road, Caleb?" she said as she backed up toward her bag. "I mean, once you get slaughtered by me, how will you recoup?"

Caleb gave a full laugh then. "A civilian outshooting me? Can't happen."

"There you go, thinking you're always right."

By that time she was by her bag. She leaned down and then ran into the surrounding bushes for cover. For the next two hours, they ran around like children until they had run out of ammo on both sides and wound up in the lake, floating and relaxing as the sun began to go down.

"You can go ahead and say it," Caleb murmured.

"Say what?"

"You know, Caleb, you were right again."

Skye peered at him through the slits in her eyes. "Are you serious?"

"Mmm-hmm"

Instead of responding, she let her feet sink until she

was standing up. Then she put her hand on the surface of the water and sliced across it, creating a wave of water to hit him. When she heard his shocked gasp, she started to laugh. He shook the water off and looked at her, laughing. Walking towards her, he smiled.

"Funny, funny," Caleb said.

Skye nodded and continued to laugh at him. When he was standing directly in front of her, she stopped laughing, stood with her feet braced apart, and looked him in the eye.

"I'm not afraid of you, Caleb Matthews," she said breathlessly.

One moment they had been head to head, and the next he had swooped down and kissed her. There was no time for her to worry, no time for her to think. He kept the kiss smooth and light. It wasn't demanding, and he made sure not to touch her anywhere else. This was about and for her. He wanted her to know she could trust him.

When his lips pulled away from hers, she thought it was done, but then she felt him press kisses along her jawline and neck until he came to her shoulder. Then he leaned his head against her shoulder and spoke.

"It's time to go," he murmured against her skin.

"Caleb," she said in an invitation to stay.

He stood up, looked at her, and then walked out of the lake. Turning towards her he said, "You look like all of my dreams right now."

"Then why are you leaving?"

"Because for once I want more than just a dream."

"What about what I want?" she asked.

Caleb held out his hand, and she walked to the bank and used his hand to guide her out of the lake.

"This is all about what you want. You're not the woman I have a fling with on the ground beside a lake. I'm not a teenager anymore. I know that good things are worth waiting for, and taking the cake out too soon means it will spoil."

He turned his back and reached for his water gun. She came up behind him and hugged him.

"Thank you," she murmured against his back.

He ran his hands over her folded hands at his waist. "So you'll know I'm no saint. For you, I want to make sure we follow the rules."

She kissed his back and then walked around him to get her gear and change her clothes. It was the first time Skye was wondering if she really wanted a prince, or a pirate.

Eleven

"I hear he was in the war, and that he killed women and children," Loretta Caulson, a member of the town council, said. Skye was in the next aisle over, restocking shelves. She was still feeling the glow from yesterday's lake rendezvous. When she overheard the two gossiping women in the next aisle, immediately she knew who the two gossips were.

"He works in the store doing stock. I'm sure he's good at counting things and hiding them," said Clarissa Nogles, the town beauty queen who was also on the town council. Skye had no love for the voluptuous woman. Clarissa was one of the judgmental people her best friend, Hannah Jenkins, had to deal with in town.

Skye wanted to jump out and confront them, but instead, she listened.

Clarissa sighed. "You know I don't like talking about anyone. I mean, I know a lot of people think otherwise, but some things need to be said. It's not personal at all. I'm doing what's best for the town."

Skye rolled her eyes. Clarissa doing what was best for the town could only happen if, all of a sudden, the town became Sweet Clarissa.

"Well, there was some talk that he wouldn't go out with you and then started up with Skye," Loretta said.

"You make it sound like I'm bitter. I don't want to have anything to do with him. I mean, I think the fact that Skye is with him speaks to how lonely she must be feeling, to take up with a stranger. He'll leave her in no time," sniffed Clarissa.

"Clarissa, let's go. It doesn't look like he's coming out to the floor. I wanted to show you the scar I saw on him. I'm sure it's something he got while killing someone innocent," Loretta tsked. Clarissa agreed, and then the two of them left the store.

Skye stood up and looked at them, heads bent together, walking down the street. She understood that new people provided new gossip for the gossip mill, but that was worse than she had expected it to be.

There was a weird race in Sweet Blooms to see who could do the "first" things with the new person. Who could have coffee with them first? Who could meet up with them on the street first? Even who would meet the person at work first. All of these things she anticipated when it came to Caleb. What was unexpected was the judgmental attitudes that she had heard, and they hadn't even met or spoken to Caleb for any extended amount of time.

Skye was determined to put the conversation out of her head until a customer caught her attention.

"Excuse me. I'm looking for a small gift for my daughter's birthday. She'll be nine," the woman said.

Skye showed her the gift section, but as she got ready to leave the customer to her purchase, the woman cleared her throat.

"I heard the new man is working here and that he has no family," she began. "I've also heard that he's quite the man to look at. Is he working today?"

"His name is Caleb Matthews, and he's a good worker," Skye said. "I didn't hire him for his looks, so I can't speak to it."

The woman laughed. "Of course you didn't, but I hear he's very fit. It must be all those guns he carries around with him."

Skye was trying to keep her smile. She realized the woman hadn't looked at the gift section at all. She wasn't in here looking for a gift, she was trying to get some new dirt and/or gossip on Caleb. Where did this need to hunt him down come from?

"He doesn't carry weapons on himself all the time. He's very smart, and he's a quiet person who doesn't want to bother anyone else."

The woman nodded. "You're probably right. He wants to keep a low profile. If all of that killing is even half true, a lot of people would be looking for him to get revenge."

Skye stopped and just stared at the woman. "What are you talking about?"

The woman blinked twice and then went on. "Oh, you didn't hear? Clarissa said one of the reasons she refused to date him is because he bragged about how many kills he had. Clarissa just couldn't go out with a man that had that many souls on his hands. She says that she's seen the signs before, and any moment he could snap and just kill everyone in the house."

Skye could barely form a coherent sentence. "You don't think you should at least talk to him? You know how things can be misinterpreted."

"No, I mean, out of the two of them, Clarissa is one of our own."

"So you've never had the experience of Clarissa or anyone else not telling you all the details." Skye took a deep breath. "When you met him, did you have a negative experience? Was he rude to you?"

"No, but…"

Skye looked at the woman, trying to gather her thoughts.

The woman looked defeated. "I haven't talked to him at all."

Skye shook her head. "You know how things can happen or how one word can destroy a person's reputation. I would hope that someone would at least meet me before they decided that they weren't going to pass judgment on me."

"I figured since he was in the service and he admitted to having a job as a sniper… You know what all the movies and stories say about that kind of man."

Skye shook her head sadly. "No, I don't know what they say. If I listened to that, then I'd have to listen to all the stories they say about small towns and narrow minds."

"I never thought about it like that."

"Caleb works here in the store, and I feel safer with him here. I think he's a hard worker and an understanding person. I think we should give him a chance because it's hard to find people who want to move to a small town without changing the way the town's run."

The woman nodded hesitantly and then cleared her throat. "It wasn't that big of a deal anyway."

Skye nodded. "Good. I'd hate to think I didn't know the people who I grew up with. To think all this time I was telling Caleb how good we are here in Sweet Blooms and how he would be welcomed for serving his country and putting his life on the line every day for us."

The woman nodded again and then looked past Skye's shoulder.

"Oh, I have to go. I see some of the other ladies that I was supposed to meet with. Thanks for talking with me."

"You had to be there," Skye said as she jabbed her milkshake. "First it was Clarissa, and she was about to call him a serial killer. Then it was followed up by that woman who decided he must be deranged or something because he was in the service. How does it happen that if a person says they're in the service, it means that they are all having problems?"

Hannah nodded as she popped a sweet potato fry into her mouth. The plate was sitting in between both of them, filled with sweet potato fries and chicken tenders.

"Are you going to eat those fries?"

Skye looked at the plate and shook her head. "I'm so confused with you, Hannah. If you wanted to have sweet potato fries, why didn't you just ask for them?"

"Because it didn't really look good until I saw it on your plate," Hannah said as she popped another fry in her mouth.

Skye shook her head and laughed. "I thought this type of behavior was reserved for Adam."

Hannah grinned as reached for another fry. "I want to make sure I share the love between the love of my life and my bestie."

"Where was I before we addressed this issue you have about pilfering fries?"

"You were defending the man," Hannah told her. "It was passionate. I think it speaks to how well things are going between you two."

"I know he's new to town, and I know that he's not what a person would call social, but I don't think he's to the point that we can start making gross judgments."

Hannah grinned at her. "I don't know, Skye. Look at all the things I went through. We both know Clarissa is, well, Clarissa. We may be hoping that the town is more evolved, but the truth is people are people. If they don't have a life, they try to find one by watching others."

"I get that, but to think he's going to wake up and be a violent Rambo? He hasn't made a scene or even a hint at it. Instead, he's quiet. He works without a problem. He doesn't mind interruptions, and he's beyond patient when I'm trying to figure out how we're going to do new things at the store."

Hannah wiggled her eyebrows. "It seems like he's turning out to be a knight in shining armor."

Skye rolled her eyes and then reached out to eat a fry. "Let's say I can see he might have had some prior training."

"Well, I for one am very glad that he's turning out to be a good candidate," Hannah said as she ate another fry.

"Do you think I'm really taking it too far? I mean, I would defend anyone who was being judged for no reason," Skye asked.

Hannah wiped her hands on a napkin and then laid her hand's palm up on the table. Skye placed her hands in Hannah's.

"Listen to me. I'm your bestie and what matters to me, is you."

"We're friends."

"You have passed the friend stage, and you are now approaching man and woman stage. Remember to be honest with, at a minimum, yourself if no one else."

"I'm telling you the same things that I'm telling myself."

Hannah gripped Skye's hands and gave her a tug. "Look deep within yourself, and when the light is bright, grab onto it and fly like the locust."

Skye laughed. "Really? You've been watching kung fu week again!"

"Hey, don't knock it. Those guys have to know something. In every movie, there is always an old man on the mountain. He's stroking the long white beard. They must have acquired some knowledge to be up there that long and have that amazing hair and nails."

Skye pulled her hands back. "Enough. I'll be careful."

Hannah tapped the table to get Skye's attention. "This man is different, and I know how vulnerable you are right now. I'm looking out for you in case you can't look out for yourself."

Skye took a deep breath and looked into her best friend's eyes. "You're right, of course, which is why I'm here, and you're the best friend ever."

Hannah patted her hand and took another fry. "So now that we've addressed that question, I have to ask the other pressing question that, as your friend, I'm absolutely required to ask."

Skye was confused. "Really, what could you ask that would be more personal than the question you've just asked me?"

Hannah leaned closer to the table and whispered, "Have you kissed him?"

Skye sat back and laughed at Hannah. "You sound like we're in high school again."

Hannah sat back in her seat and laughed as well. "Don't think you're going to throw me off like those other people. I see you haven't answered the question."

Skye rolled her eyes and then grabbed some chicken.

"Really, Skye, do you think I don't have enough patience to wait while you eat? This is the juicy part."

Skye looked at Hannah and grinned. "I don't remember asking you these kinds of questions when you were getting together with Adam."

Hannah waved a fry in the air. "No, you didn't. It was a missed opportunity on your part. I, however, will not be missing this moment. So 'fess up. Have you?"

Skye hoped she wasn't blushing. "Yes, we have kissed."

"And?"

Skye looked up at the ceiling as if the answer would come to her. "It's magical, as corny as it seems."

Hannah smiled. "No, I understand. It's still magical with Adam, so I completely understand. Well, it looks like this new man is on his way to getting a princess."

Skye nodded and grabbed her milkshake. Through the rest of their conversation, Skye thought on Hannah's words. Skye was thinking Caleb might not be on his way to getting a princess, though—he already had one.

Pierce was impatient waiting at Skye's front door. He hoped he would get a chance to talk to Skye by herself. Situations were getting out of hand. Pierce had called all the vendors, and every one of them had received a call from Robert. He had put in a lot of time trying to get this gig with Cade Designs, and he knew if he could just work this deal, he would be in with a larger clientele. Failure wasn't an option. It didn't matter the way it was done. It only mattered that the endgoal was accomplished.

He waited and then rang the bell again. He was about to use the knocker on the door when Skye opened it up.

"Pierce?" she asked, confused. "I thought you were someone else."

"I'm sorry to disappoint. I can go if you want?"

He knew she was disappointed and wanted him to go away, but her common decency would force her to do the right thing. Instead of telling him to go away, she put on a smile and motioned for him to come in.

"Your houseguest?" Pierce asked.

"I don't know. I thought you were him actually."

Skye led him into the living room. Pierce looked around, and the whole scene looked very rustic to him.

"I see you like the country décor," Pierce said. "It's very bold of you to stay with a trend that isn't at the height of fashion anymore. I think your choice in decorations speaks a lot about you as a woman, bold and on the forefront."

Skye had on her cut-off jeans. She was about to go for a walk. Her hair was pulled back into a ponytail, and her tee shirt was stained with paint and other household projects she had tried to do before.

Skye sat down in an oversized chair and give Pierce a wry smile. "I'm not sure if I've been complimented or insulted."

Shaking his head vigorously, Pierce went on. "No, no offense was meant. I was trying to compliment you in a clumsy way. I was trying to say that you are bold and take charge. I find that it is a part of your personality that I really like." Pierce plastered on a smile. He had to be careful. Skye was friends with someone from the city, but it appeared she actually chose to stay in this town. He could see he had some work to do because she had chosen the chair farthest from him and sitting close wasn't an option.

She looked like a reasonable person. Pierce's figured that since she was a store owner, they would have some basic grounds to be able to talk on. In retrospect, he was finding that the pursuit of money was not a primary goal of a lot of store owners in Sweet Blooms. This kind of thinking only confirmed his thought that, eventually, Adam Cade would come back to the city. He would return and remember the project manager who came out to see him while he was in the middle of nowhere.

"So, Pierce, why did you come all the way out here to talk to me? Is there something wrong?" Skye asked.

"Yes, yes, let's get straight to the matter. I'm afraid I came out here for some advice. Regarding the storage matter."

Skye sat forward. "Tell me what the issue is. Robert is really good at these things. Do you want me to call Robert and ask him to come over now so we can all talk?"

Pierce held his hand up. "I'm sorry, Skye, but the issue may be Robert, and that's why I came out here to get your advice on the matter."

"Well I'm sure whatever you think is wrong is simply a misunderstanding."

What Pierce really wanted to say was, "Can't you keep that old man under raps? He's trying to mess up my gig." However, he could see from the amount of concern that she showed towards Robert that that wouldn't be the way to go.

"I'm sure you're right. I feel like some of the issue may be because I'm not from Sweet Blooms. I was hoping that things would be different, but I think I'm still seen as an outsider—and one from the city no less."

Skye agreed. "Sometimes people can be a little narrow-minded, but I think after they get to know you, you'll find that they generally want to help you. So tell me the issue."

"I went to Robert because he can hold my supplies, but it seems like he's investigating every one of my vendors. He calls them and makes sure the quality of all of the supplies is correct. I appreciate his helping, but I think he's making my other vendors feel like they aren't trustworthy. I only found out because one of the vendors called me on the side and wanted to tell me that the other vendors felt insulted."

Skye stared at him in disbelief. "That doesn't sound like Robert at all. Did you ask Robert why he was looking?"

Pierce could hear the concern, but it was for the wrong party. How did anyone get anything done in this town? There was no offer on her side to speak to Robert. There was no question about if this would affect their relationship and the money he was paying her. Pierce could see he was going to have to take a different approach to this situation.

"What can you tell me about him?"

Skye smiled. "Robert is a native of Sweet Blooms. He's had a home here all of his life. He left when he was straight out of college and went into the military. He's never been married, and he has no kids. He came back and did some security work for people in town when we started getting more tourists showing up. He also does some construction management and building in town. He's the head of the local woodworkers and others who have hands-on skills. It's not official, but Robert is really good about organizing them and getting them together."

"Oh, I see," said Pierce. It was becoming all too clear how Robert was in his way. The phone rang, and Skye excused herself. Pierce kept his face serene but inside he was boiling. This couldn't be. He couldn't be this close to getting a break, and have the thing that was in his way was a good ol' boy. When Skye returned, Pierce decided to try another tactic.

"I'm sorry, Pierce, you were saying?"

"What I'm saying is that Robert could be costing me money. I know everyone must like him, and he's from Sweet Blooms, but he's scaring my vendors."

Skye sat back and seemed to emotionally pull away. Her smile was wiped off of her face. "There must be something wrong with the vendors then."

"Skye, has anyone reviewed his work? I feel like he's reviewing mine. I'd like to know I'm working with someone competent. I know you said he had prior military service. Does he suffer from PTSD or something?"

Skye's expression tightened. "I think we should stop the conversation here, Pierce. I understand you are a little nervous, but Robert is as good as gold."

Pierce stood up with Skye. "Please, Skye, I'm not being critical. I'm coming to you as a friend and a business person. This kind of interrogation can be misinterpreted."

"Interrogation? He asks some questions, and they feel interrogated?"

"Perhaps you're right. I'll reach out to my contact and try to allay his fears." Pierce could see the relief on her face, and it made his blood boil.

"Good. I think that's the best thing because Robert is rarely, if ever, wrong. Look at what he does as a benefit to you."

They walked to the door. Pierce turned at the door and smiled at Skye. "You're right. Thanks."

"I'm glad I can help. I'll see you when the next shipment comes."

The door closed and Pierce put on his glasses as he went to the car. He would go to the hotel and think about how to fix this Robert problem. He was too close to losing it all now.

<h1 style="text-align:center">Twelve</h1>

"He makes me think there's a real difference between country and city folks," Skye said as she dug into her macaroni salad. "He didn't call or even give me a hint that he was coming."

Caleb was massaging her feet on the couch. When he had arrived, Skye was in a snit, but he didn't know why. He'd planned a scheduled moment, but she said she didn't want to go anywhere, and he agreed. He said he wanted her to lay on the couch as he massaged her feet. At first, she was hesitant. She ran upstairs and washed her feet. It took everything in him not to laugh out loud. After a few moments, and him getting her some food, she was relaxed and spilling out her frustrations for the day.

"Are we talking about here at the house or at the store?" he asked.

"Both! He's so uptight. He thinks about everything in terms of how other people see them. He actually said my house was out of style. He implied that I was taking a risk with the decorations in the house. Then he went on to talk about Robert and how he must have PTSD or something because he was questioning him. I think he expected me to say something against Robert."

"Then he doesn't know how fiercely loyal you are."

Skye smiled at him with her spoon mid-mouth. She ate the macaroni on the spoon and then pointed at him with it. "You're good, Matthews. I didn't see that one coming, but it was on time and smooth."

"Thanks. Us knights in training have to practice when we can."

"I love running the store, but I don't like dealing with business people like Pierce."

"Is it a real problem, or is he just a nuisance?"

Skye thought about it and took another bite of her macaroni. "It's the store I love, and meeting and helping the people. I tried to help him too, by getting him and Robert together. What I'm trying to say is that I thought I did a good job trying to help him and now I feel like he's throwing that back in my face."

Caleb continued to massage her feet, moving up to her calves. "You did your best. I know it's your nature to try and help everyone and everything, but you have to be able to move back from people and things you can't help."

Skye sighed. "I want to be a good neighbor. If he's having problems with Robert, then I feel as though I'm also a part of that problem."

"I didn't know you were that omniscient or all-knowing."

"What?" Skye said.

"I'm just saying taking the blame for two grown men not getting along, that's a bit above and beyond the call of duty."

Skye looked at him and agreed. "You're right. I need to have some more perspective. Okay, let's talk about something else so I can put this on the back burner.

This whole thing with Pierce, and then some gossip I heard in the store, made me think about you."

"You heard gossip about me? I haven't been anywhere," Caleb groaned.

"Obviously, that's not completely true. It's all over town that you snubbed Clarissa, the town beauty queen."

Caleb stopped massaging her leg and then looked at Skye. Then a memory dawned on him. "Oh, I think I know who you're talking about. I was doing my cool down at the park, and a very attractive woman came by."

Skye raised her eyebrows. "She was very attractive, you say?"

"She must have been because she had that Marilyn Monroe breathy voice."

"Hold up, how could you not know if she's right in front of you?"

"Easy. I was doing tree pose to find my balance after the run. It's harder to do yoga poses with your eyes closed, and I usually do them with my eyes closed so I can get the fullest out of my workout."

Skye laughed. "So let me get this straight. You never opened your eyes?"

"Nope. It would have messed up my routine."

Skye started to really laugh then. When she had a grip on herself, she motioned for him to go on with the story.

"Anyway, I heard this woman with the sexy voice. She came to me and said something to the effect that my arms must be so big because of all of the guns I've carried."

"I told her, 'I know I have a great metabolism, and I build muscle up quickly.' She went on to talk about how she was part of the welcoming committee."

"Yes, she was trying to welcome you alright."

Caleb smiled. "Anyway, she went on to say that if I needed any midnight help, because I had served my country that I could feel free to call her. And I let her know when I feel the night tremors come on me, I go hunting or running for long hours. I heard some giggling and a hiss, and then she left."

"Well, you left quite an impression, and when I heard Pierce today, it was the first time I really noticed how prejudiced people can be against people in the military. When Pierce implied all military people had PTSD, I realized how ignorant it sounded, and I wanted to apologize to you if it ever seemed like I had thought that about you."

Caleb smiled. "Does that mean that Pierce is out of the picture?"

"I never said Pierce was in the picture."

"We won't quibble over me being right again," Caleb laughed.

"Fine, let's not quibble. Did you come over to rub my feet? Not that I'm complaining. I didn't realize how comforting it would be."

"No, I came to share a moment with you."

Skye stopped laughing. "We share all the time."

"We do, but you're waiting to see if I'll become your knight. I've already chosen."

"Caleb—"

"Don't worry, princess, I'm not rushing you. I just wanted you to know. So, as you know, I was in the service. One of the biggest things we had to have between us was trust. When I met Stephen, I realized I had chosen a job that didn't require me to trust anyone. I could save them, but I never expected them to save me."

"Caleb," Skye whispered and reached out to touch him.

"Don't frown, your brother was right, and I needed to be more trusting. So I want to share something with you."

"You have me on pins and needles now."

Caleb tapped her leg and flashed her a smile. He stood up and reached for her hand. "When I was in one of many foster homes, I graduated, and one of the foster mothers taught me how to dance for my prom. I never made the prom, but I remembered how to dance basically. Will you dance with me?"

He saw her hesitate, and for a moment Caleb wasn't sure what she was going to do it. Then she unfurled from the couch and took his hand.

"Music?" she asked.

"I'll hum. It will help to make sure no surprise moves are thrown in there," he said with a smile.

He reached out and placed his hands around her waist. "Come closer, princess. I've taken a shower and brushed my teeth," he said jokingly.

Her fingers curled around his shoulders, and everywhere that she touched, she left a trail of warmth that reminded him why he needed her. When he brought her into his arms, he felt like a missing piece had found its way back to him. He didn't even want to move, much less dance, but he'd said they'd dance, and he wouldn't break his word to her, ever.

He started to hum and gently sway back and forth. She was stiff in his arms, and he looked down to see her gaze frozen on his arms. He blew her hair, and it made her look up.

"This is supposed to be my dance, not the last requiem before an execution."

She looked away sheepishly. "Well, since we're confessing, I can't dance."

They both stopped.

"You didn't go to prom?"

"I did with Stephen. He didn't want anyone to bother him because he wasn't really into anyone at the time, and no one bothered me because I was Stephen's sister."

"Well, then, this presents a grand opportunity for us to dance the way we want to. I personally like to take the lead. Do you mind?"

She looked at him, confused. "I just told you I can't dance, so what do I care?"

"Good, bowing to my better idea is always a good place to start."

"Whatever."

"Step on my feet."

"Excuse me?"

"Step on my feet so we can dance."

"I'm not a kid."

"I know that, but it will be fun."

Reluctantly she stepped onto his feet. Once she did, he started to move and go in circles. She held on tighter to his shoulders and started laughing.

"I don't think this is the way it goes."

Caleb moved in circles effortlessly through the living room. "I don't know. This is working for me. It's just like I thought it'd be on the floor at prom."

"If you were really like this, you would have run into everyone and knocked them down. Slow down," she said through her laughter.

"I assure you the book I read and the woman who was kind enough to teach me said for me to cover the whole room."

"Okay, Fred Astaire, stop. I'm getting dizzy."

When they stopped, they were laughing and out of breath in each other arms. He knew he was playing with fire, but when she was around, he threw caution to the wind. He had her in his arms, and he was pulling her in for a kiss that he knew would change things. As his head inched closer, Skye's phone rang, and the song 'Girls Just Wanna Have Fun' blasted through the moment.

"Ugh! Ignore it," Skye murmured. Then Caleb continued his descent, but the phone blasted again.

He rested his head against hers. "You might want to ignore it, but someone really needs you."

Skye picked up the phone and Caleb was nearby just in case.

"Hello?"

"Skye? It's me, Hannah."

"I knew that from the tone."

"And you hesitated. We'll speak on that later. I hope it was for a knight." Skye smiled, and Caleb grinned.

"It was and is."

"I hate to be the party crasher, but I need you."

Immediately Skye straightened up. "What do you need."

"It seems as though there's been some drama with Pierce, and Delilah is distressed. It has to do with how things are being handled. I need a native who's not upset who can translate for me."

"I'm on my way. You at the ranch?"

"Yes."

As soon as Skye pushed the end button, Caleb offered to take her to the Cade's place.

"Sorry we had to interrupt our dance," Skye said.

"Don't be sorry, princess. This is another side of you

that I adore. You're faithful to your friends. I hope all is okay, and if you need anything, let me know."

He dropped her off at Cade's and then went back to the house. When he walked in, the memory of them dancing stuck with him on the cold evening run.

"I can't die yet, I haven't finished," Skye said as she fell onto the grass. She was wearing her tank top with jeans today. "This is the last time I believe Lucy when she says it's just a little project."

She had her hair up in a ponytail, and she was wiping her face with a rag from her back pocket.

"I know you've done this before. Cleaning up a lot for your store," Caleb said. He was eyeing the other people who had come out to help Lucy clear the land and get it ready for the construction crew.

Caleb marveled at how the town had sent out a few telephone calls yesterday, and they had all rallied together to help Lucy out. It wasn't the most organized affair. He had to step in more than once and tell people where to put items, but he was happy there were bodies to redirect to new places. The men had shown up and moved the debris. The women had also shown up with food in hand to help serve.

"I've done this before, but I didn't like it then either. It's the kind of work that you feel good with after the fact," Skye said. "By the way, in case no one else has told you, thank you for showing up and putting in the time and organizing the people."

Caleb smiled at her and kept an eye on the group. Every now and again he had to step in with an older gentleman called Jerry. He was trying to pick up items that were a bit too much for him. He had to find all sorts of ways to help him out. It appeared that his wife Geeta was there as well, and she thanked him out of Jerry's earshot for being there.

"With this as a warm-up, I don't suppose you want to go for a run?" Caleb asked.

Skye fell down like a starfish on the grass. "I can't even believe you would mention something so offenisive to me. A run? Why aren't your arms all jelly like the rest of us?"

"I've been carrying things that might have been a little heavier."

"Well, I have a better idea," Skye said.

"You do?"

"Yes, I think we should take one of those scheduled moments of yours."

Caleb smiled. "Are you saying that you scheduled something for us to do?"

Skye sat up and smiled right back at him. "What I'm saying is that I spontaneously scheduled something for us to do just now. So you see, I scheduled it a full five minutes ago."

"Fine. I said I would help them tie up something and then we can leave. I think by then, everyone will be winding down anyway."

Skye agreed, and Caleb took one long look at her walking to the picnic tables before going to meet with the rest of the guys.

Two hours later, Skye and Caleb were sitting under a tree with a hodgepodge of a picnic basket. Skye had liberated a tablecloth for them to sit on and then gotten the other ladies to donate some food for the cause.

Though truth be known, the contributions didn't start coming until Geeta stepped in and told everyone how grateful she was to Caleb.

They were both in their work clothes. When Caleb had suggested he drive them home, Skye said no. It was spontaneous, and they'd be fine.

When he eyed the tablecloth, he complimented her. "You must have been a great girl scout. Always be prepared, or at the very least, improvise accordingly."

Skye tilted her head in acknowledgment. "You are so right, dear sir."

She handed him a sandwich, and he passed out the water bottles.

"I have to say it wasn't me, although I'll take some credit. This was the least I could do in order to thank you for coming," she said. "It's times like these that I remember why I love being in Sweet Blooms. When one of us has a problem, we all band together to make sure we are good. It doesn't matter what is going on in the town either."

"I saw that, and thanks for making me a part of it." He stopped chewing and gave her a long stare.

"What?" Skye asked.

"I'm just wondering, are you really that good?"

"What kind of question is that?" Skye asked.

Caleb leaned back and took another bite. "Well, you have to look at it from my point of view. You don't swear. You don't drink. You don't smoke."

Skye interrupted him. "Hold on right there, buddy. I know where this is going. I want you to know I have lots of bad habits."

"Really? Well then, tell away."

Skye laughed. "I leave dishes in the sink at night."

Caleb put his hand to his mouth and opened his eyes really wide "NO! It can't be you leave dirty dishes. I wasn't even sure you ate food."

"Just stop it," she said, laughing at his ridiculousness. "I jaywalk."

"I think that was retired from the list of bad things because everyone does it now."

"I'm bossy."

"You?"

"Okay, well, maybe you don't think I am, but I had it on good authority from Stephen that I was quite bossy."

"Maybe you've mellowed in age."

"Are you saying that I'm old?"

Caleb laughed at her indignant look. "Don't worry, you'll always be a princess to me."

"Hello, Skye." She recognized the smooth tone of Pierce's voice.

Skye couldn't believe it. She didn't know if she should be concerned that Pierce was a stalker or not. She had heard other people say how some city folks were just too pushy for their own good. She always thought they were exaggerating, but now that she was here and Pierce was looming over her, she had to give it a little more credence.

When she shaded her eyes and looked up, she saw Pierce in business casual. Who wore business casual all the time?

"Hi, Pierce."

Caleb wiped his hands on his pant leg and then gave him a salute from his seat. "Hey, how are you doing, chief?"

Pierce looked between the two and his brow furrowed. "Aren't you an employee at the store?"

Caleb smiled. "Yes, that would be me. Mr. Do-It-All at the general store. I'm surprised I even caught your eye, Chief."

Pierce stood for a moment and then let out a small sigh. He descended to the tablecloth and then looked at them. It seemed to take him a minute of looking at the tablecloth before it came to him what it was. Shaking his head, he turned to Skye.

"Have you given any thought to the topic we were discussing before?"

Skye let out a huge sigh. "I don't think there's a topic to be discussed."

"I should hope you've looked into it to see if there was any merit to my concerns before dismissing it." Pierce turned to Caleb. "Certainly you can help in this. I was concerned about Robert, being that he is prior military. He may have some issues that make him unstable to work with or can cause paranoia. He seems to be exhibiting paranoia with my vendors."

"Has he exhibited any behavior to make you think so?"

"He's calling all of my vendors and questioning their integrity about the product they are sending to Sweet Blooms."

Caleb shrugged. "I wouldn't worry about it. If that's all he's doing, then it's probably not that he has a problem but more like this is just who he is."

Pierce gave him a second glance and then shook his head. "I think he's just from a small town, so he doesn't get it. He doesn't have the exposure to understand how money is made is the real world of big cities. Vendors in large cities deal with large accounts all the time. If they even take these accounts into the smaller regions, you should be happy for the acknowledgment and business."

Skye watched Pierce try to convince Caleb of what he wanted to say. She had to say Caleb was handling it so much better than she did at the house. If she went by Caleb's expression, they could have been talking about anything, but definitely nothing as important as what Pierce thought it was.

"If they think that Robert is too much of a hassle, then I would tell them to walk away now."

Pierce's lips pursed. "I don't think you should be here discussing business with owners. You're just an employee, after all."

"Hold on, Chief. I do think I should be here."

"Really? I didn't know we let staff members contribute to the decisions of the company." Pierce deliberately turned from Caleb. "Exactly who is this person to speak for you in business affairs?"

Skye had watched the whole scene unfold, and still, she was having a hard time keeping track of the banter. What could she say that wouldn't sound disparaging to Caleb? She didn't really want to deal with Pierce, but she knew he needed a response. There were other things going on that she wasn't at liberty to talk about with Pierce. It was becoming a hot mess.

Thankfully Caleb answered before she had to. "While it's true I work at the store somedays, today, while we're here, I'm the man in Skye's life," Caleb said with quiet authority.

Pierce stopped and paid Caleb some attention. "What did you say?" he asked incredulously.

Caleb smiled. "She's the woman, and I'm the man in her life."

Caleb reiterated the words so slowly that Skye almost laughed, and she knew she was probably blushing at the same time. He'd named it, put it out there. It was no longer something nebulous.

Pierce looked between the two of them and smiled. He gave a small chuckle. Skye heard it, and at that moment she was nervous. When Pierce looked up at her, he had a confused look, but he looked her up and down and then shook his head.

Caleb reached over and touched her hand. At that moment she was never so glad for another person's touch. "Be careful, chief."

Pierce shook his head and looked more confused than before. "You've traveled the world in your profession. You decide you want to settle here, and like this?"

Skye felt the wind taken out of her. She hung her head, blinked back hot tears of shock, and swallowed the hurt that had been slammed her way. It was verbal, so there wasn't a reason to attack him. She didn't have the verbal agility to come up with something witty to say back to him. She wanted to just fall into the ground and hope that when she came back, Pierce would be gone, Caleb would forget, and that it had somehow not happened at all.

"You know I do have a form of PTSD. It makes me extra protective of women and children from things like you. I have to forgive your ignorance. If you had been around the world like I have, you'd know that I'm hoping that Skye would settle for someone like me." His hand tightened on hers, and he looked at where they were both touching. Then he looked at Pierce. "I've seen your kind before, Pierce. You go to a place that you think is beneath you and you try to dazzle people with new things you have. You don't understand that everyone has a value, and that value has nothing to do with you. It has to do with them being unique. Skye is precious to me. She stands up to me. She calls me out when I'm wrong, and she's faithful to her friends and family. I know those things are hard for you to understand because they're so foreign to your nature."

Skye heard him, and she had to concentrate on keeping her mouth closed. She knew he was doing it because he wanted to protect her in front of Pierce, but she would remember this time always as the day she fell hopelessly in love with him.

Pierce looked between the two, and he nodded to Caleb. "Well played, Caleb. I can see I've come too late for her to see any reasoning in regards to business. I won't waste any more of my time. I'll be leaving."

Skye didn't even notice when Pierce left. She was looking at Caleb, and she hoped all she felt wasn't written on her face.

"Wow," she whispered.

"Really? I think I should have hit him, but I couldn't think of a way to do it without doing long term harm. Then if I was asked if I meant it, I would have to say yes. It was complicated. I thought combat was done in close quarters."

"I've been trying to address him, but it's been difficult."

"He's desperate."

"Really?"

Caleb looked over at her, "Oh, get that *poor Pierce* look off your face. I don't want you to feel bad for him at all. He chose the way he's going, and it's going to bite him in the rear when it's done."

Skye put her hands in her lap and let out a deep breath.

"Caleb, it could be true. You have been everywhere. I've only been here in Sweet Blooms. I mean, at one time I was naïve enough to think Pierce was a nice guy. I'm not saying everything he said is true, but there is something to be said about how I'm not in the same class of experience that you are."

Caleb moved closer to her and pulled both of her hands into his. When she tried to pull her hands back, he held firm.

"Look at me, princess," he whispered.

Skye did, slowly. When her eyes found him, she was mesmerized by his gaze.

"You've been in Sweet Blooms, and you've had a wealth of experiences I've never had. You're smart, funny, and brave. You met me and took me in on my word that your brother had sent me. Don't make too much of my traveling. Consider that a majority of my time was spent in hiding watching people, not actually interacting with them. Your character speaks volumes for you, and I'm hoping to catch up. You should be so proud of who you are and proud of where you come from."

"I am," she whispered. "But I'm human, and there are days of doubt."

"Pierce is running around like a chicken without a head. He's looking for someone to help him, and it's like I said before—he's desperate."

"You're right, he's desperate, and even though I think he's a heel right now, I feel bad that he's in a bind."

"You can only help someone so much. Pierce doesn't appear to be the kind of person who wants help unless it's on his own terms. If you want to go ahead and try to help him, fine, but remember you can only help those who want it."

Thirteen

Skye should have known it couldn't last. Yesterday she had discovered she was in love. Maybe she didn't really need a knight. Having a Caleb was even better. As if he could read her thoughts, he showed up at the store and brought some boxes from the back so Cassandra could place them on the shelves. He gave a small nod and then went to the back. In the background, she heard the bell of the front door, but it was background noise next to seeing Caleb.

"Hello, Skye." This voice was the voice that had killed many relationships. It was Clarissa, the beauty queen. Skye shook her head and stood up tall.

"Hello, Clarissa."

"I've come because I needed your signature and figured we could do it over coffee. I have another meeting there in about ten minutes if you don't mind?"

Yes, I mind, thought Skye, but she buckled down her inner five-year-old and nodded. Clarissa led the way out of the shop. When they had taken a seat inside the coffee shop, Clarissa pulled out the papers.

"The council wants to thank you for supporting the festival. It's businesses like yours that make it possible for us to do the festival in a way it should be done to represent our town. I trust you've spoken to Hannah about the festival as well."

Skye knew that question was coming. Ever since her best friend had gotten together with Adam Cade, the town rich boy, everyone tried to get her to talk Hannah into supporting something. If Hannah supported something, Adam would give money to it.

"I can't say that I have, but I'll definitely get to it. You wanted me to sign some papers?" Skye prompted Clarissa.

"Oh, yes, here they are."

Skye looked over the documents and confirmed the numbers in her head. When she was on the last document, Clarissa started to talk.

"I was surprised that you still have Caleb around."

"Really?"

"I didn't think he'd stay around. You know how people talk."

Skye knew it was bait, but she couldn't let it go. "People will always talk."

"Yes, well, you know how they talk. People can be so mean. You're right. I just wondered how you were dealing. I mean, I recently spoke with Pierce. He told me some nonsense about you and Caleb being a thing. I told him it couldn't be true because you know what it's really about."

Skye signed it all and then gave the papers back to Clarissa.

"I know what it's really about? I think I'm confused here."

Clarissa smiled and leaned in.

"You know what they say about those soldiers. They

find someone to help them heal, and then they leave. They can't really acclimate to small towns and people like us. I mean, if he stayed, he'd probably be here out of duty and guilt because he was with your brother. I know you're not the type of woman to keep a man that way."

Skye knew her smile was still in place because Clarissa's face fell.

"You're absolutely right. I'm not the type of woman to keep a man against his will. Thank you so much for the information and for bringing the documents for me to sign."

"Well, okay. Maybe we can—"

Tapping her wrist, Skye walked away. "So sorry I can't. I'm so busy getting ready for the fair."

Skye walked out into the street and didn't see a thing. It was true she could see Caleb doing something out of guilt and duty. Hadn't he said she needed to trust her friends? She had totally forgotten that Caleb had been there with her brother. Guilt and duty! The words were like daggers to her heart. What had she been thinking? She should have known that he was here because he was doing the right thing as a good man. Even yesterday had been him coming to her rescue.

Skye walked into the shop. She didn't see anyone. She kept her smile on her face and went straight to the back of the store. She had been waiting for a knight in shining armor, and he had arrived. She had to stop this and let him be free.

It didn't take long for him to follow her into the back. When she looked at him, it was one last time with him as the knight.

Skye took a deep breath and let it out. "Caleb, I want you to know that I really appreciate you coming to

Sweet Blooms, delivering the note, and fulfilling my brother's last request," she rambled out. "You've been so helpful to me, making me able to remember him and not cry."

Caleb smiled, but he had a bit of a confused look. "What's wrong, princess?"

Normally, that endearment would have her smiling. Today it was a reminder of how much he was doing for her. She stood up tall and clenched her jaw. She could do this. "Well, I have you to thank for this. You have gone above, and beyond the duty you were tasked with. I think that my brother is satisfied and we don't need to go any further."

He walked around the room picking up boxes and stacking them in the correct places. "So what brought this on?"

"It's something that hit me out of the blue. It's only natural that we became friends because we both knew Stephen, but anything else would make things unclear."

"Oh, I think they're pretty clear."

Skye started shaking her head. "No, I think it's just been too much."

"Let me see if I understand. You think that I've been, what, forced to like you? Was I reading this wrong and you didn't feel something between us? I thought we trusted each other, princess. You think it was—"

"I think you've been great. I think when people stay in close proximity, it's easy to misread things and they become other things that really shouldn't have been," she countered.

He stopped moving boxes and leaned against the wall. "Are you going to tell me what happened?" he said through clenched teeth. "What was the gossip?"

Skye looked at him, coiled in perfect anger against the wall. His body was tense. His pose was deceptively relaxed against the wall as if nothing was bothering him.

"What gossip?"

"So you're not going to tell me?"

"Caleb, I think this is the best way. I also think you should leave by the end of this week. If you aren't leaving town, I can always talk to the hotel owner, and he can give you a good rate until you decide what you're going to do."

"You left with Clarissa this morning, and you came back another woman. What did she say?"

Skye wanted to tell him, but if she did, he would do the right thing, and it would be the worst thing for him. He shouldn't be saddled with her. Caleb was an amazing man, and he deserved the very best, not an emotional trap. "I told you, I think this is the best thing for you…and me."

"I think you need to think on this and remember the first rule," he said to her. "We're in it together." Caleb looked like he would say something else, but instead, he grabbed his coat and walked out the back door. Skye watched him go. When the door closed, she just sat down on the stool and let the pain take her.

She still had a shop to run, so there would be no moaning now. This she knew how to do. Work and smile now, go home and mourn later.

Skye was numb. When she came home, he was gone. He hadn't even waited for the end of the week. It was like losing someone all over again. When she walked through the house, she saw him everywhere. When she went into the living room, she remembered the two of them dancing. When she went on her walk, she remembered him saying he was always right.

She knew it was the right decision because he hadn't bothered to call her in three days. During those three days, she had justified her actions to herself and her pillow. She knew she'd done the best thing for Caleb. Taking advantage of him by parlaying his good nature into a relationship had been horrible. It was better that she saw the truth of it all before he got hurt.

The words sounded right. The problem was those words were cold at night. She felt lost and lonely without him. There was no place she could go now because it had all been visited by him. He had left his mark on her and her life. She was ashamed to admit it hadn't been this bad when Stephen had passed.

Skye tried to fill the days until she was exhausted. Hannah had been trying to reach out to her, but she'd found one excuse or another not to meet because she knew as soon as she saw her, the dam of tears would fall again. Late at night, she wondered if he thought of her.

She knew it was going to hurt when she had decided to let him go, but she had scheduled in time to gradually do the process. She was going to wean herself off of that straight-talking guy. In the days that passed, she realized she hadn't just lost a knight—she'd lost a friend.

What was the real problem?

It was true she was concerned that maybe Caleb had let his concern go from pity to caring. At night she wrestled with what had been the issue. On the third day, she knew what it was. She was intimidated and scared. Caleb had been just about everywhere on the planet and done just about everything. She was scared that he would wake up and realize she was a small-town woman. She lived in a small town, and she'd probably die in a small town. The thing was, she was happy living in a small town. She might want to visit the rest of the world, but that was it. Would it be enough for him? Or would he say it was nice, but eventually not want to play house anymore?

These were the thoughts that plagued her right before she went to bed. She got ready to turn the lights off so she could go through another restless night when the doorbell rang. Skye hesitated. What if it turned out to be Pierce? The bell rang again.

"Skye, I can see you haven't turned the light off. I want you to open the door. I have my key, but I won't use it unless I'm welcome."

At first she stopped, and her heart jumped for joy. Was he welcome? Was she, crazy? Of course, he was welcome. Then common sense doused her enthusiasm. What did he want? Was he here to tell her she was right and to confirm all of her misgivings?

She went to the door and opened it up.

She didn't know what to expect. It definitely wasn't a drenched in sweat Caleb at the door. He looked amazing. She wasn't into the sweaty look, but she was into the Caleb look. A dark tee shirt that was matted to his chest. Shorts that went to his knees, and well-shaped calves that said he was in shape from head to toe.

He was breathing heavy but staring at her. "Tell me you're done thinking about why we won't work, and you'll listen to me?"

"Listen to you?"

"Yes, listen to me. Remember, I'm right most of the time," he said smugly.

Skye stood with her hands on her hips. "Maybe you're right a lot of times, but everyone can be wrong at least once."

"Give me a shot at what happened?"

"Caleb—"

"I think what happened is busy-body Clarissa came into the store. I know because I saw her. Then you two went to the coffee shop. She started saying some craziness about us not having a real relationship, that it was all based on pity and duty. I got that one two days ago when I heard her gossiping about it to another woman. All of that might make sense, but I'm still lost on why would you believe her. You know what kind of woman she is."

She bit her lower lip. "You had to be there," she said quietly. "It seemed so reasonable."

"It seemed so reasonable coming from the woman I won't date or be caught alone with? Meet me halfway, Skye."

Skye stood in place and stamped her feet. "I feel like a kid. I feel like I need to protect myself from you leaving me."

Caleb stepped closer. "I know you think you're not enough, but you have to trust me when I say you are. I think you're amazing. You think you haven't done anything, but everyone knows you in town. I respect you, and I care about you. And I have to tell you, to see you in this Betty Boop nightshirt is just the sweetest thing ever."

When he stepped towards her, she went into his

arms, and they kissed as if they hadn't seen each other in years. She clung to him and held on like she'd never let go. He cradled her as if she were the most precious person on the planet.

He drew back and stared into her eyes. "Tell me you missed me, princess," he murmured. "I hope you did, because I missed you like I've never missed another person before."

She stared back at him for a moment before she spoke. "I missed you, but I was scared. I was too scared to hear the truth. I thought if I just let you go, I would have done the right thing and then I'd never have to know if it was true that you would get bored with me."

"Never would I get bored with you. You might drive me crazy and put me in a tree, but other than that, you're good and stuck with me."

"What do we do now?"

Caleb laughed. "I know you must care for me because I'm a sweaty beast and you haven't complained about my smell yet."

Skye laughed. "When the euphoria fades away, I'm sure I'll faint, as is appropriate."

"Will you indulge me tonight, princess?"

Skye smiled. "Yes."

"Good. Go sit on the couch. I'll give you a massage, and you can confess those pesky insecurities to me."

Skye stopped and looked at him. "Really?"

He bent down and kissed her on the forehead. "Really. I don't know who I missed more—my princess or my friend."

Skye propped herself on the couch, and they turned out the light. While he massaged her feet, she spoke of the things that made her feel insecure and doubtful. He didn't judge or offer ways to fix it. He just let her talk it out. She couldn't tell when, but at some point she fell asleep. It was the first real rest in three days.

145

<h1 style="text-align:center">Fourteen</h1>

Hannah patted down the seedling in her garden, then sat back and looked at Skye sitting on the bench.

"I can't believe it," she said. "Every time that we saw Pierce, he seemed to be kind and jovial. When we asked if he needed any help, he always said no, that he had this."

Skye was trying her hand at knitting. Hannah swore by it and gardening. Gardening wasn't her thing. "Well, I think he was handling it by calling all of his friends from the city and asking them to take on vendor contracts."

"It wasn't so much that he was breaking the agreement when it came to vendors. Not to say that it isn't a big issue. I think the other issue is that all of the equipment is substandard or just barely up to building grade."

Hannah was meticulously writing out the name of plants on white plaques that would go into the ground. Skye had watched her more than once, and she found the exercise exhausting just to watch.

"It's a good thing that Robert gave me a call," Hannah insisted, not really happy that she needed someone to contact her so she could discover how Pierce was mishandling the management of the woodworking project.

"Robert is very understanding, and he's a local. You know everyone has only nice things to say about him. To think that makes him an anomaly..."

Hannah flinched when Skye said Robert was a local. "Are you saying that I should let a stranger take care of the woodshop instead of me doing it?"

"Now, now, Hannah, don't get all sensitive while you have me out in this heat trying to tie some knots with two sticks."

Hannah opened her mouth, and nothing came out the first time. "Knitting is very therapeutic. I thought I'd do the project."

"So let me be clear—no."

Hannah laughed. "Well, sugarcoat it, won't you?"

Skye looked at Hannah through one eye. "By the time I get this knitting thing down, I'll be called one-eyed jack." Hannah decided to save her friend.

"So, me managing the project is a no-go, but who then?"

Skye watched Hannah clean her hands and then pick up the knitting she had been trying to do for the last hour. In moments she had the first knot on the needle, and the first six stitches were done.

Hannah gave the knitting back to Skye. Skye investigated the handiwork and then replied, "Show off." She put the craft next to her and looked at Hannah.

Skye shrugged and asked, "Why don't you just ask Robert to do it?"

"I want someone else besides him. I just don't know him well."

Skye nodded. "Well, there is another far-out idea I have."

"Hit me."

"Why don't you ask Delilah? I haven't seen Adam's grandmother around town a lot. We know she knows how to run a woodworking shop."

Hannah smiled. "Now that's an idea that will work. Lately, Delilah hasn't been around as much. I wasn't sure if she was having a problem with me or what."

"With you?" Skye asked incredulously.

Hannah shrugged. "It could happen. As the people say, I'm not a native here."

Skye went to Hannah and hugged her. "You can be a native by association." She pulled back and looked her in the eye. "I think Delilah will love the challenge. She can work with Robert and all will be well."

Hannah tossed the idea around in her head. "I think that will be a great idea."

Delilah Cade looked at her duffel bag on the bed. Delilah knew this day would come. Adam would get his own family and move on. He would start new endeavors and make new friends. Most importantly, he wouldn't have time for her anymore.

She had been randomly coming to Sweet Blooms. There were some people she could visit, but she had nothing to do. Adam had fallen in love with Hannah, and she thought it was the best thing in both of their lives. Hannah was a hard worker with a son. Hannah didn't need the advice of an old woman.

Both Hannah and Adam were working on a career.

They had scheduled to be engaged for about a year before they got married. That meant she had, at minimum, a year before she heard the pitter patter of little feet running around. Until then, she was going to go back to the city and not be a nuisance. Of course, no one had said she was a nuisance, but no one noticed if she was gone or not. She would just go home until they had kids. Or someone had kids.

A soft knock tapped on the door. "Ms. Delilah, may I talk to you?"

"Please come in." Delilah watched Hannah come in and once again was so grateful that she had come into Adam's life.

"How can I help you,?" she asked. She didn't want to dawdle because she didn't like goodbyes either. She was trying to figure out what kind of traveling she would be doing to eat up the time.

"Adam told me you were going to leave," Hannah said. The girl had come into the room and closed the door. Delilah prepared herself. Maybe she was going to tell her to stay away. One of her other friends from the center told them it had happened to her. Her grandson had gotten married, and the new wife told the grandmother she needed to pick a home or a full-time attendant because the random visits were going to stop. At any rate, Delilah wasn't one to complain, she would deal with whatever came.

"Yes, I mentioned it to Adam. I didn't want any kind of fanfare."

Hannah took a seat. "I'm glad that Adam told me because I would have had to fly to New York to speak to you."

Now Delilah was intrigued. She looked for the

nearest seat and settled in to hear what had to be a grand tale. Hannah was wringing her hands so it must be something that was weighing on her mind.

"I don't know if you heard about the incident with Pierce?"

"I heard some of it, but I confess, I didn't avail myself of all of the details."

Hannah nodded. "Well, let me tell you. Adam had to hire a project manager for the woodworking house. He picked Pierce because he had all the qualifications. Unfortunately, Pierce couldn't abide by the rules we set. We want to build the house, but it should be with local talent and local sourcing for building materials. We were told that Pierce hadn't bothered to use any of the local talents and was selling the contracts to less than reputable people."

"Really? Did Adam lose any money? You know you have to look into the contracts and see if he's committed us to anything." Delilah saw a large smile break out over Hannah's face.

"You know, Ms. Delilah, I'm so glad you mentioned it. The first thing is, I have no idea about that kind of thing. More importantly, I don't want to know anything about that sort of thing. The reason I came here is that I'm hoping you'll help us in this crisis."

Delilah was confused. In truth, Hannah was very forward most of the time, so this long road to asking her something was a bit nerve-wracking.

"Hannah, I'm unclear. What do you need from me?"

"Well, I was hoping that you'd consider being half of a team to manage the project."

Delilah laughed. She immediately covered her mouth. "Hannah, I am very flattered that you asked me, but I don't think you understand the industry of woodworkers and craftsman. While the rest of the world has advanced into the twenty-first century, they haven't. That is to say, I can talk to them, yes. I can even get a couple of them to do something for me, yes. But when it comes to contracts, negotiations, and other items in their day-to-day that affects their money, I don't think I'll be the one to help you."

"Adam and I talked this over, and we wanted to pass it by you first. We understand that the industry is not as advanced as we would like it to be, so we wanted to know if you could work with Robert from the general store. Have you seen him? He's the very quiet guard."

Delilah didn't have to think hard. Of course she'd seen him, with his piercing eyes and grey temple hair. He was a fine man. He was also fit, and she hadn't seen him flirt or gossip while she had been in the store. Not that she had been looking or anything.

"I think I remember the man," Delilah replied.

"Well, he's the representative for the craftsmen in Sweet Blooms. He also happens to do a lot of work in town on construction. He was the one who let us know that none of the projects were making it to Sweet Blooms. He was also the one who found out all of the vendors Pierce used were people who had bad reputations; they were people who used sub-standard equipment."

"So I'm still not clear. You want me to work for him?"

Hannah smiled. "No, you two would be equal partners in all decisions. I just think it's important to have someone to represent us in this project. After the debacle of the Pierce incident, I'd like one of us, so to speak, to be watching this project as well."

"Well, it does sound like a very big task."

Hannah went to Delilah's side and picked up her hand. "I know you would be able to bring so much to the table if you did this. The other thing is, we want you to stay around, but I know things can get dull. If you choose to accept, we'll go offer this to Robert. Or, if you want to hold off giving us an answer, you can go to Robert and ask him how he feels about working with you. I think that's the better idea. The two of you will be together a lot, so it's probably best if you go check out your chemistry."

Delilah almost fainted when she said chemistry. Delilah took a deep breath and then patted Hannah's hand. "Don't worry. I'll reach out to Robert tomorrow, and then I'll be able to give you an answer."

Hannah jumped up and hugged her. "I knew I could count on you to try. Thank you so much."

Hannah left the room, and Delilah pulled out a handkerchief to wipe away the tears. She wouldn't be going home alone. She wasn't being put away. They still wanted her. She took a moment to review her options, and then Delilah made a decision. She would find Robert, and he would work with her. That was it. He just needed to be informed.

Fifteen

Skye was relieved that she and Caleb had talked and that he was back at the house. It was the end of the day, and the tourists had been pouring into the store. They were here for the festival, and this year it seemed like there were more of them than there was last year.

As she looked around the store, she noticed it looked like a Black Friday sale had happened there. She saw Cassandra bustling around the store and Skye was grateful for her. She was looking forward to going home today. On top of everything else, she needed to make sure things were crystal clear between her and Caleb.

After fifteen minutes, she waved goodbye to Cassandra, who said she would leave as soon as she fixed the toy section.

"Cassandra, you have to get out of here. We can finish cleaning in the morning."

Cassandra laughed at Skye. "I'm good. I start to wake up after one in the afternoon. Besides, I just want to fix the toy section. The toys you get from the woodworker are amazing. His toys sell so well. I'd love to meet him."

Skye nodded to the now empty space where Robert usually stood. "You need to let Robert know. He knows all of them. He brings the shipments in weekly for them. I think tomorrow, or the day after, one of the craftsmen will be at the hotel because he's bringing in a larger shipment for the fair."

Cassandra's eyes lit up. "Maybe I'll get to meet him then. I sound like a groupie. Go on, I'll see you later. Hopefully, when I meet the artist, I won't embarrass myself."

Skye got into the car and let Caleb drive them to the house. She was grateful that he was here today, but also apprehensive. She didn't know where he got his energy from. At some point, he had changed into his running clothes. She knew he ran every night before going to bed, but she thought today would be an exception, as busy as they were. If his clothes were any indication, that wasn't going to be the case.

"Hey princess," he said. "You're thinking so hard that I can hear you from over here."

The night had fallen when they pulled up in front of the house, and Skye was beyond exhausted. She was back home. She and Caleb were back home, and Skye needed to make sure her refuge was really that.

"Princess?"

She got out of the car and stood in front of it. She didn't want to wait until after his run. She grabbed his hand and walked him over to the beginning of the path. She knew this seemed like a crossroad.

She wanted to make sure she was clear, and all was well. She realized from their last discussion that she had made the both of them suffer because she hadn't been upfront or honest. She wasn't going to do that anymore.

She was going to be strong enough to put everything out there and be upfront. Last night when she thought about having this conversation, something in her cried out to leave well enough alone. Caleb deserved all she had and a part of that was being honest.

"I think we should talk," she said.

Caleb gave her a lopsided grin. "Somehow you have managed to start the conversation with one of the scariest phrases to all men everywhere."

"It figures. I don't think it will be long. I won't hold you up too much from going on your run. Okay?"

Caleb shook his head. "I'm not committing to anything until I hear what you have to say."

Skye smiled. "You're a smart man."

"Thank you, but I'm not smart, I'm just cautious about committing. You have to be that way when you're with a princess who thinks faster than you."

Skye gave a chuckle. She had to say this to him and make sure the slate was clean, but now that it was time to deliver the speech, she was less than ready to do so. Stephen had always said she never trusted gifts. He told her that when someone gave her a gift, even as a child, she often gave it back and waited to see if they really meant for her to have it. She took a deep breath and then pulled on her proverbial big girl undies.

"I wanted to clear the air," she said. "I know things were getting real close between us as the days have gone by. Things just happened, and there wasn't really a long conversation or an understanding of where things were or what we were doing."

Caleb smiled. "Ah, I see, said the blind man. Do you want me to help this—"

Skye held up her hand. "You may know the answer,

but this is one of those messages that I have to say, and then we can go on from there."

Caleb motioned for her to carry on.

She wrapped her hands around her midriff and then dropped them to her sides. "You have done everything and then some that Stephen asked you to do. In fact, you've been here and helped me in ways that I didn't know I needed. So I want to officially say that I thank you for coming on Stephen's behalf, and any and all obligation you had to Stephen has been fulfilled. He couldn't have found a better person to do it either."

She waited for his reaction. He didn't fall on his knees and yell that he was free at last, so that was a plus. Instead, he was very still, and his face was impossible to read as he spoke.

"So we're saying that the connection between us is over?" he asked.

She nodded.

"From this point on, you would agree that my duty, as you call it, to fulfill my best friend's last request is at an end?"

"Yes, that's what I'm saying."

Caleb had a large smile on his face. "I'm so glad you're finally where I am. So let me tell you this—we are an item and have been for a minute. I know you don't like it when I say I'm right, but—"

She was confused by his ramblings. "Stop! What are you talking about?"

"I'm talking about making sure you know we're together. You know, going steady. You're my gal. We're an item and all the other euphemisms people have." He leaned down and gave her a kiss on the cheek. "You know, now I can do that in public without people thinking we're sneaking around."

She smiled from the tingles that ran down her spine. She needed to hear the rest of it, though, so she pulled herself away from the pleasure. "So, to be clear, you're okay with being with me and no one else?"

Caleb shook his hand in a fifty-fifty motion. "I don't want the 'you're with me, and I'm with you' kind of thing, and we just linger on that way. I want something more exclusive and permanent."

"Exclusive dating?" she asked.

"Oh yes, there will be exclusive dating. I'm going a little farther though."

Skye was excited and scared at the same time. It was like Christmas was coming early because it couldn't wait for the end of the year. "I want to bring to mind that we are already living together."

Caleb took a step closer and pulled her into his arms. "It's true we've gone out of order, but I think we've done the dating, the 'we have problems we should talk about' stage, the 'are our families compatible' stage, and the 'do we still like, respect, and care for each other after all that has gone on' stage."

Skye was floating in the euphoria of his arms. "Okay, what is it that you want?"

Caleb reached out and put his fingers under her chin so he could see her face. "I'm thinking we should enter into the 'let's get engaged' stage."

Skye looked into his intense gaze, and her vision was clouded by tears she tried to blink back. "If you're sure."

Caleb smiled. "Of course I'm sure. I told you, I'm always right."

Skye leaned into him and whispered, "I do think there is just one more thing we need to do for Stephen."

Hannah was lying on Adam on the couch in her living room.

"Things happen, and we can't read everyone correctly when we meet them."

Adam was feeling down, and he was angry with himself.

"I messed up, Hannah. I was the one who hired Pierce. The thing that really bothers me is that I chose Pierce for all of the wrong reasons. I knew I was picking him because he was from the city, and I gave him more credit than the local talent."

Hannah wanted to tell him these were people he knew, and that his decisions were logical and that anyone could have made a mistake. She knew he wouldn't take to those answers, though, because he had come to Sweet Blooms to settle down based on what his gut told him. And when it came to picking a project manager to build his woodworking shop, he had ignored his gut and gone with business.

Hannah stroked the arm that was holding her to his side.

"Adam, what's the real problem? I'm sure when you were wheeling and dealing in the city you made some choices that you regretted. Did you take all of them like this, or did you just look at them, solve them, learn, and go on?"

She could feel him take a deep breath.

"Hannah, the reason why this one bothers me more than the others is I think I was prejudiced."

Hannah sat up and looked at Adam.

"What are you talking about?"

Adam ran his hands through his dark hair.

"Yes, I think that at the end of the day what I did was look at the city manager and decide that he had more experience delivering the top-notch quality I was looking for. I thought the local talent might not be able to think big enough to make my woodshop amazing, so I went against my gut. That was bad, and I did it for all of the wrong reasons, and that's why I'm feeling ashamed."

Hannah got up on her knees and moved in closer to Adam. She reached out and ran her hands over his trimmed beard.

"Listen to me. When you did his reference check, did that go well?"

"Yes, everyone said he had a great record," Adam muttered. "No one had caught him in anything, and they all said he was well connected with vendors."

"What that tells me is you went about this the right way. It may be true that you didn't think the local talent could deliver what you wanted, but that wasn't the only reason. If you feel that you weren't as open minded as you should have been, then fine. Let's look at it, identify it, and we can be on the lookout for it if and when it shows up again. What's important here is that we realized we made a mistake and learned from it."

Adam pulled Hannah into his embrace.

"So you're not going to beat me up for having that city attitude?"

Hannah shook her head. "No, I'm not. We all have pain points we need to work through. Now you know that one of your points is making some prejudgements. What's important is you found out, and we've got a pretty great solution to this issue. We'll do better next time, and both of us will be on the lookout for this."

"Prejudice and not trusting myself. I'm starting over again, and I didn't want to fail in front of everyone."

"Listen, if you want, we can come up with a whole list of mistakes, but I think we need to focus on what we got out of this. I think it's important that we were able to turn this around and get Delilah to help."

He leaned in and kissed her on the neck. "For that, I can't thank you enough. I knew she was going back and forth, and she seemed like she wanted to leave. I didn't know how to ask her to stay. I know she has friends in the city."

"She has friends, but family is very important to her. I think we've been a little wrapped up in ourselves and we haven't been as attentive to our family. Nathan left me a note with his picture on it."

Adam smiled. "What did it say?"

Hannah rolled her eyes and laughed. "It said, do you remember this person? He lived here six years ago, and he wants to reconnect."

"Ouch!"

"Yeah, so we both have some things to work on. What matters is that we are working on them together."

It was the beginning of fair week. Skye's shop was listed as a hot spot this year where tourists could find unique objects, and she was also participating in the town scavenger hunt. To say there were a lot of people in the store was an understatement. Robert had to "help" more than his share of people out of the store discreetly. It was a policy that Skye didn't arrest shoplifters if they were kids, but she reported them to their parents. Fortunately, they didn't have a large problem with shoplifters but as the town picked up business, she saw it more. Robert assured her he would give her some ideas to help them out.

Skye looked over the packed floor and saw Caleb showing people around. She was so happy that just looking at him made her smile.

"Oh my goodness, Skye, are you mooning over the man?" Cassandra teased. "I don't know if I can work in these conditions. My boss in love with an employee. What will happen next, the security guard finding love on the town council?"

Skye rolled her eyes. "Whatever, and I didn't say I love him."

Cassandra gently touched her on the shoulder. "You didn't have to."

Skye walked over to Caleb to see him explaining one of their more popular toys to a young boy.

"See how the box opens when you put in the right combination. Isn't that awesome?"

The boy nodded his head, intrigued. "How many combinations are there?"

Caleb smiled. "You'll have to find out when you play with it."

"Thank you so much," the mother said. "It's so hard to find toys that aren't electronic for kids today. We had heard about these toys in town. I just had to bring my son here to see if he'd find anything he'd like."

Caleb smiled. "We're happy to help. The toys are

made by our local craftsman, so if you have any problems, let us know."

Skye tapped Caleb on the shoulder. She didn't even need to say anything; he just turned and guided them to the back of the store. When they got there, he closed the door and leaned against it.

"Finally, I've got you to myself," he said, reaching for her.

Skye went into his arms. "Did you want to skip out for lunch? I imagine every place must be packed, though."

"I planned ahead and picked up some sandwiches from the Banter House this morning. Of course, not all of them made it. I needed some sustenance after the morning run."

She laughed at him, and Caleb retrieved the basket that was on the shelf. Now that they were official, she got to revel in his company. There were still some moments when she thought it was still too good to be true, but then she reached out and pinched Caleb.

"Did I tell you how happy I am that you're in my life?"

Caleb smiled. "No, but you should probably tell me now before we do our run tonight."

Skye moaned. "The run? Maybe we should discuss these runs of yours. Who runs when there's no one running after you?"

Caleb laughed. "You run now so when and/or if something ever runs after you, you know you won't be last."

Skye held up her hands. "Okay, I give up. I'll try to do the run, but I think we should do the modified run. I need to work up to what you do."

Caleb grinned. "Of course."

"By the way, don't forget, no run and no surprise getaways tomorrow. I want to do something that I think will be great for us both."

"You've been saying that, but you haven't said what it is."

Skye smiled. "I know. It's a planned surprise."

"Hey, good job. Those are the best surprises ever."

When they left the room, they walked right into two female customers who took one look at Caleb and immediately needed help. Skye paused for a moment and then she went to help another customer. She knew Caleb cared for her, and he was an attractive man. It was only natural other women noticed him too. She was going to have to decide to trust that he wouldn't just wake up one morning and decide he was tired of her. Did she think he was that flaky?

Skye jumped when she felt a hand on her shoulder.

"Hey, where did you go?" he asked.

"I got thrown by the impromptu entourage."

"You know it means nothing. I've already got my princess."

"What happens if you decide you'd like to try some concubines? I know we're together, but I guess I didn't realize this was going to be a part of our relationship that I need to deal with."

"I know you don't know it, but you're beautiful. When men look at you, I remind myself that you care about me, and I say too late, man." Caleb shook his head. "I'm so fortunate you chose me. At the end of the day, that's what keeps us together and faithful. We chose each other."

Sixteen

Cassandra was beyond excited to come and look at the leftovers from the toy craftsman. He lived in the hotel when he came by with his goods. She knocked on the door and heard him say, "Come in!"

He was sitting in a tee shirt and jeans at a small table that looked like it was meant for two little girls to have tea at. "Excuse me, I'm Cassandra from the general store. Skye sent me over to look at your items."

He looked up and stopped. He placed the toy he was filing on the table and went to look at her more closely. When he was within three feet, Cassandra took a step back.

"You have the most amazing lines," he said, appreciatively.

Cassandra laughed. What exactly did a person say to that? "Thank you. You are?"

He didn't hold out his hand but instead angled his head to the right and the left, looking at her face. "I'm Evan Sparrow. Can you lift your hair up for a moment, away from your neck?"

Cassandra had heard about eccentric people, but this would be the first time she would actually be around one, and she had to say it was a bit disconcerting. She nodded and lifted her hair.

"Absolutely beautiful."

Cassandra swallowed and let her hair fall back down. "I—um, thank you. I know you're working, and I don't want to be the one to interrupt, but I wanted to know if you had any time to show me any new items. Or would you rather I come back at some other time?"

"No, no, you can look over on the other table. I've got samples on the table that you can touch. If you like any of them, let me know, and Robert will bring the rest of them down depending on the quantity."

Cassandra went to the table, and she was instantly entranced. He had new toys on the table. There was a multi-colored box that had movable parts and sported a sign that said Open Me. There was a dragon that sat on a sign that said 'I can be a car as well. Can you figure it out?' Then there were some 3-D items, like a hand that could be used to hold pens, and there was a nameplate that looked like it was coming towards you. She touched each piece reverently.

"You like it?"

Cassandra jumped when she heard Evan's voice. Then when she remembered why she was there, she smiled.

"I have to admit, I think your work is pretty amazing."

"Really?"

Cassandra could see he had no idea how much his work really impacted a lot of kids.

"We always sell your stuff, and we usually have more requests than we have product. I think it's a great thing that you make toys for kids that makes them use their minds.

Not that videos and technology can't do it, but you don't see a lot of toys that make children reason and use their hands to get something done. There's something to be said for a person who builds something with his hands."

Evan nodded. "If you make it with your hands then no one can take it from you."

Cassandra nodded. Okay, that wasn't quite where she was going with it, but he was the artist, so she could go along with it as well.

"I'll tell Skye what I saw. Do you want me to give the order to Robert?"

"Yes. Did you want to see how and where I make my toys?"

Cassandra stopped. "Now?"

"No, I mean I could arrange it if you wanted to see them."

Cassandra looked at him, and there was an uncomfortable pause before he jumped in and said, "Nevermind. I'm sorry I asked. I just thought… Well, it doesn't matter what I thought. You can tell Robert, and I'll make sure you get what you need."

Evan walked away and went back to his table to start filing away on his latest creation. Cassandra was confused. When he first invited her to come and look at where he worked, she thought he was trying to flirt with her maybe, but then he backtracked so quickly that she wasn't sure exactly what had happened.

"Well, I'll be leaving now, Evan. Thank you so much for letting me see your work."

He didn't look up; he just grunted and then nodded.

Cassandra took her leave with haste, thinking Evan might be talented, but he was not a social person.

It was a perfect day. Skye had told Caleb that she wanted the both of them to do something this Saturday, but she hadn't told him what. Like clockwork, he was at the front of the house at 9 a.m. When he saw her, he smiled. He was dressed in a blue shirt and khaki pants with some loafers.

"I see we have on different clothes today," she teased.

"Well, I tried to take the middle road. You see, I have a planned surprise today, but no one told me what I should be wearing, so I had to make my best guess."

She tapped him on the shoulder. "You did good. I guess I have to give you these planned surprises when I want to get you out of jeans and your shorts."

He pulled her into his embrace and gave her a kiss. "Or you could just tell me where we're going, and then I'd know how to dress."

Skye smiled up at him. "I could, but where is the fun in that?"

She took his hand, and they started down the path.

"We're going on a walk?"

"Yes."

When they got to the juncture where they ran every day, Skye made a turn in a different direction.

"You haven't taken me here before."

"No, I haven't, Caleb. Don't worry, I won't let any of the ferocious animals have you," she joked.

They continued to walk until the path emptied onto a wide open space. They were still on her land but it was a sacred place. It looked like a garden until you got closer and could see the white tombstones. Skye looked at the headstones. She kept each one clean and tidy. Every space had its own flowers.

She looked over her shoulder. "I know this isn't a normal, fun date that people go and do, but I thought this would be a good place to confirm our start and close up old things."

Caleb looked around and then hugged her. "Thank you for bringing me here. I know how much this place means to you, and how much the people here mean to you."

Skye blinked back the tears. "It's a family plot. My parents are here, and two of my aunts. Stephen was brought back here too."

She held out her hand, and they both walked hand in hand until they were standing in front of Stephen's grave.

She let go of Caleb's hand and knelt down to Stephen's grave.

"Hello, Steph. I wanted to come and thank you. Thank you for knowing me so well that you sent a knight to save me. Thank you for being an example of what it means to love selflessly. I wanted you to know that I finally found what mom and dad had. I found someone who can love me just the way I am.

"I wish you were here. I wish you had been here to see me happy. I know wherever you are, you are always looking over me. I love you, big brother, and I hope you find mom and dad on the other side."

Just as she was getting ready to rise, Caleb touched her shoulder, and she looked up. Tears were streaming down her face, but she didn't try to hide them. This was Caleb, and he was going to be her other half.

"May I?"

Skye nodded. Caleb joined her, kneeling.

"Hi, Stephen. I think you tricked me and I fell for it. I remember all of the things you used to say about your sister. For a long time, I thought she was some made-up apparition. I didn't think the woman you described could actually be true. You spoke about her so much, I was sure I was in love with a dream. When you sent me here, you knew how broken I was, and you still gave me the greatest gift a person can receive: love. I owe you big time, and I'll never be able to repay it. But I promise to do everything I can to make Skye happy. Watch your six until I get there."

By the time Caleb was done, Skye didn't even bother to stop the tears.

They both stood up, and he wiped away her tears.

"Don't cry, princess."

"That was beautiful."

"That was the truth. I know there will be ups and downs, but as long as we still love each other and are open and honest, we'll be fine."

She stepped away and held out her hand.

"Together?"

He grabbed her hand and kissed it. "Together."

Check out book four of the Love Happens series *Sweet Dreams* and read Kelly and Joshua's story.

Sign up to my newsletter to receive updates on new releases, sale promotions, and free books.

susanwarnerauthor.com